THE LAST OF THE
ARMAGEDDON WARS

THE LAST OF THE ARMAGEDDON WARS

RALPH DENNIS

BRASH
BOOKS

ISBN: 1941298826
ISBN-13: 978-1-941298-82-4

Published by
Brash Books, LLC
12120 State Line #253
Leawood, Kansas 66209
www.brash-books.com

PUBLISHER'S NOTE

This book was originally published in 1977 and reflects the cultural and sexual attitudes, language, and politics of the period.

CHAPTER ONE

It was a dogleg flight. The thigh was in the Midwest and the foot was South.

P. J. Turner flew into Washington from Detroit. There was a two-hour wait before the flight to Atlanta. The second part of the trip hadn't been scheduled in Detroit. That ticket had been one-way to Washington. It was an easy enough matter to find the Eastern counter and buy a first-class ticket to Atlanta. He booked it in the name of Paul Tibbets and paid cash.

P. J. Turner wore muted gray plaid slacks and a blue blazer. He was an inch or so over six feet. His long, thin face was topped and overshadowed by sandy red hair. There was a deep cleft mark in his chin. His eyes were flat dark beads behind sunglasses.

The Eastern flight landed at Hartsfield International in a light rain. It was the last day of April, a Friday. Seven o'clock and there was a lot of daylight left. It was, he knew, because of Daylight Savings Time. That uselessness. It meant nothing to him in his business.

The cab that took him into town passed Atlanta Stadium. Signs above the stadium parking lot announced: *Braves vs. Phillies 7:35.* With the window open, from the sounds, he knew that the game was underway in a light drizzle. The parking lot was about half empty and P. J. Turner could understand that. He followed baseball and he knew that the Braves were returning from a four-game series against the Mets. They'd dropped all four games. Except for the hand luggage he carried, and the fact that the "new" Braves were just like the old Braves, he might have had the driver drop him at the stadium. It would, under the right circumstances, have been a good way to spend an evening in a new town.

By the time the cab reached downtown Atlanta it was raining harder. He knew the game was washed out, done. It was that kind of heavy rain. Later there'd be thunder and lightning. It would be a good night for sleeping.

The business was still three or four days away. Two days to study it and plan it. To walk and think it through. To find the weak place and the way in and out. The way in was no good without the way out.

P. J. Turner was thirty-six. In the eight years since he'd been on his own, since Bill Grace had made his dead mistake in Louisville, he'd carried out twenty-six hits. Only one of the twenty-six had lived after he walked under the gun. He hadn't lived long. Four days. It was one of the best records in the business.

Bill Grace had taught him well. Before he himself forgot what he'd taught.

The taxi dropped P. J. Turner in the driveway of the Peachtree Motor Lodge. After he paid the fare and the cab moved off, he stood on the steps that led to the lobby and looked around. It was like he counted to sixty twice. Then, carrying his single piece of hand luggage, he entered the motel to register.

As soon as the lobby door closed behind him, a black Plymouth eased to the curb across the street. Two men got out. One wore a tan trenchcoat. The other had on a dark blue raincoat that might have been Air Force issue some years back.

"It was a good guess," the man in the tan trenchcoat said. His eyes were not on the motel. He was watching the taillights of the cab that had dropped off Turner.

"All of them stay here," the other man said. "Word of mouth all over the country."

They crossed West Peachtree in the driving rain. The man in the tan trenchcoat gripped something round, tubular, in the right-hand pocket of his coat. It rattled as he walked. His hand around it, it had a muffled sound.

The room was on the fourth floor. P. J. Turner closed the door and placed his bag on the bed. He walked to the window and looked down on West Peachtree. Heavy traffic down there, hiss of tires and the glare of headlights though it wasn't completely dark yet.

Not a night to be out.

He returned to the bed and unlocked and opened his bag. There were three shirts on top. He stacked those in one hand and was turning toward the dresser when there was a knock at the door. He dropped the shirts on the bed and swung the door open. Two men stood there. Both wore raincoats with dark soak smears from the rain.

"Yes?"

"What brings you to town, P.J.?" the man in the trenchcoat said.

"I don't know any P. J. I'm Paul Tibbets."

"That's what the registration card said." The man in the dark raincoat opened his hand and showed his shield. "I'm Franklin." He tilted his head toward the man with him. "He's Baylor."

"What do you want with me?"

"You don't know?" The man in the dark raincoat stepped into the room. "Give his bag a toss."

"I know my rights," P. J. Turner said.

The man in the tan trenchcoat passed him. "From Detroit, right?" He kept his right hand in his pocket. With his left hand he dug down into the bag. When he brought his right hand from his coat pocket he said "What's this?" to cover the muffled rattling. He thrust his right hand into the bag. When he pulled it out there was a pill bottle in his palm. He turned and showed it to his partner. "Pills. My guess is it's speed."

Blue raincoat said, "I hope you've got a prescription for those."

"Being from out of town," the man in the tan trenchcoat said, "I guess he doesn't know our drug laws."

P. J. Turner waited. It wouldn't do any good to protest. It was a box.

"Some of the roughest in the country. This could get you two years if you go before an unfriendly judge."

The man in the trenchcoat held the pill bottle toward the light and seemed to be counting. "All our judges down here are unfriendly, especially to people bring drugs in from out of state."

The man in the blue raincoat touched P. J. Turner on the elbow. "Ride downtown with us."

⚜ ⚜ ⚜

At the police department they photographed him and took his prints. He was charged under the Controlled Substances Act and allowed to make bail. When he walked out of the lockup the same two men were waiting for him. "Mind if we walk with you?" P. J. Turner didn't answer.

When they reached the main entrance, the black Plymouth was parked there. The man in the tan trenchcoat opened the door to the back seat. P. J. Turner looked in and saw his piece of hand luggage on the far side of the seat.

"The plane to Washington leaves in about an hour. We did you a favor and booked you a seat. You get to pay for it"

P. J. Turner got into the back seat. The man in the tan coat closed the door.

At 11:23 the Eastern flight left for Washington. P. J. Turner was on it.

Atlanta Stadium was dark when the Plymouth passed it on the way back to town. The parking lot was empty. The sign now gave the game time as six p.m. It would be a twilight doubleheader the next day to make up for the rained-out game.

Franklin drove. Baylor, with his wet trenchcoat over the seat-back between them, seemed half asleep.

"I guess that's it," Franklin said.

"The hell it is." Baylor opened his eyes and blinked at the light. "That's the start of it." He held out an open hand. "Let me see that paper again."

The paper was regular typing size, 8½ by 11, with a rough pencil drawing on it. It had been found, folded and carefully creased, in the center elastic pocket of P. J. Turner's bag.

Baylor unfolded the sheet and studied it under the soft light from the glove compartment. It showed a junction of two streets, one building with an X marked on it, some parking lots and the cluster of other buildings. After a minute or so Baylor refolded the paper. "I think I've got it."

"Who? Who was supposed to be the bloodmeat?"

"The Man."

"The shit you say."

It was something to think about. The Man, his name was really Warden Pike, ran the black rackets in Atlanta. That was the girls and drugs and the "bug" and some of the other gambling. Blacks had been at the well first and they had a lock on it. Whites had come in late and they'd hacked out their slice. It wasn't as if there'd been an agreed apportionment. It had just worked out that way.

"Why now?" Franklin said.

5

"Confusion," Baylor said. He fumbled for the pocket in his trenchcoat and shoved the drawing in. "It's the right time for it."

Both understood the reference to confusion. The election of a black mayor and the appointment by him of a black commissioner of public safety had started it. The splits and fractures in the Police Department. The petty revolts, the back-biting.

And the commissioner had put his iron hand on it. Intelligence, for which both Franklin and Baylor worked, had felt it too. They'd lost their autonomy. Now it was all through channels. Everything. And most of the police, even if they didn't resent the power of the commissioner, felt that he was too concerned with statistics that showed that urban crime was going down. Even if it wasn't.

"The word's got to be passed," Franklin said.

"Up the line?"

"To The Man," Franklin said.

"It could be a bloodbath."

"Either way."

In the distance they could see the spotlighted gold dome of the state capitol. Baylor got out his pack of smokes. The first cigarette he pulled out was damp at one end. "How do we pass it?"

"Not directly."

Baylor tore open the pack and found a dry cigarette. He lit it and blew a long curl toward the partly opened window on his side of the car. "Come up with something."

"The fat man," Franklin said. "What's his name? Was a cop some years back. Now he plays back-alley games."

"Jim Hardman."

"That's the one."

Baylor considered it. He bounced it from one side of his head to the other. "Might be. Word is he's been involved with The Man off and on."

"You just walk up to Hardman and say…?"

"No," Baylor said. "Find a pay phone."

❧ ❧ ❧

I'd been at the game. It had been a night out for my girl, Marcy. We'd hardly found our seats before it started raining in our popcorn. An inning or so later, the rain was heavy and I'd said, "Screw this," and we'd driven by Happy Herman's and bought some cooked ribs and some potato salad and gone to my house for a picnic.

Now it was dark in the bedroom. There was a slice of light from the partly opened bathroom door. The talking on the phone had awakened Marcy. She was propped up on a folded pillow listening.

I let the man talk his way through his story. All that about P. J. Turner being run out of town. That guess that Turner had been in town to off The Man. The caller wasn't anybody I knew. I'd have recognized that hoarse, smoker's voice.

"Why tell me?"

"I thought you might know who to pass this to," he said.

"Who are you?"

"That doesn't matter."

"It'll be the first question gets asked," I said.

"A friend," the man said.

"It's the kind of information that might be worth money."

"You spend it," the man said. "I'm independently wealthy." He hung up.

I dropped the receiver on the base and stood up. I found my boxer shorts on the floor next to the bed. I shook the dust off them and started dressing.

"Jim?"

"It's some rotten business," I said. "I've got to go out for an hour."

It was still raining. I could hear the brittle patter of it on the leaves of the oak outside the bedroom window.

"You want me to wait?"

"Yes." I put a knee on the bed and leaned over her. "I think that's a good idea." Her mouth was open. I kissed most of her bottom lip by mistake and felt her move her head down to meet me full-mouth. I backed away, and when I couldn't find my T-shirt, I dug another one from my dresser.

I made two calls. Hump said he'd be by in twenty minutes. The second call was to The Man.

"P. J. Turner?" The Man wore white linen slacks, flared slightly, and a crimson quilted smoking jacket. He didn't seem to age. He seemed frozen in time. That same hard-assed black that we'd met three or four years before. The same odd way of talking as if English was a foreign language that he had learned from listening to records. "I don't recall ever hearing the man's name."

"The way the man on the phone talked I thought he might have some reputation."

He stood, half posing, at the end of the coffee table. He looked comfortable. I wasn't. I'd stepped into a puddle in the parking lot at the back of the building where The Man had his secret apartment. Now I could feel wet socks and water squishing between my toes. My raincoat and Hump's had been draped over a chair next to the round, tiered bar that filled the center of the living room. There was enough booze stocked there to throw a Teamster party.

He'd changed the facing on the bar since the last time we'd been in his place. Now there were panels of black velvet. Taste was not his strong point. Power was.

"Who was the man on the phone?"

I watched the rainwater pooling under our raincoats. "I don't know. There wasn't any way to get his business card."

"Does anyone know this Turner fellow?" The question wasn't directed toward me or toward Hump. His two bodyguards, his guns, were in the room. One stood with his back to the door that led to the stairs. The other, lighter skinned, lounged with one elbow on the bar counter. He lifted his elbow from the bar and nodded.

"He's supposed to be the best there is."

"What does that mean?"

"He scores hard and fast," the black said.

I picked up my glass and Hump's and headed for the bar. The black there met me halfway and placed the glasses on the bar. He ducked under the opening at the end. He held out the bottle of thirty-year-old Hines and I nodded.

"Where is Turner now?" The Man asked.

"On his way to Detroit," I said.

"I have some trouble believing this fairy tale," The Man said.

"Don't bail out too soon," I said. "It's got a good ring to it. At least it's the way it ought to work. In the best of all possible worlds. Here's this cop from Detroit Intelligence, just happens to be in the airport on some other business. He sees Turner there. He tags Turner to his plane. Then he calls Intelligence in Washington. That's just to be sure that the flight to Washington isn't a red herring. A man from Washington Intelligence meets the plane and tails him to the counter where Turner books for Atlanta. The cop in Washington passes the word to Atlanta. Two Intelligence cops meet the plane here in Atlanta, follow Turner to his motel and roust him. They toss him good and put him on a plane and tell him to go home and stay there."

"I don't see how this involves me."

I told him about the drawing, the layout of the area.

"Was there a scale drawing of the inside of the apartment?"

"He didn't say." I had a sip of the Hines. It was almost too smooth to drink. "I'd guess not. Otherwise, I think he'd have said so."

"Then I can assume it would have been an outside hit?"

"In the street or in the lot," I said.

"That other time Jim warned you it might be that way," Hump said. "That somebody could sit on a rooftop and wait for you to come down the back steps."

I had warned him. That had been the first try, the other time they'd tried to take it away from him. The talent hadn't been that good and one had lost it trying to get up the stairs and the other one, found staggering down the street a few blocks away, had died in the operating room with about half his gut blown away.

"Thank you, gentlemen. I appreciate your help."

I stood up. Hump looked at the Hines in his glass. He'd been surprised by the curt dismissal.

"I hope that your business affairs are going well." The Man had read Hump's surprise. Now he was softening it.

It was a kind way of saying it. Asking if there were still jobs for us on the dark side of the world. Our kind of jobs. The only kind of jobs we seem to get. What you got when you were on the low side of the seesaw.

I'm an ex-cop. Forty-four my last birthday. Pudgy and sneaky. The way I left the force they'd like to forget I'd ever been there. Hump Evans is a black mountain of a man. Six-six or seven and two-seventy or so. A few pounds over his playing weight when he was a defensive end with Cleveland. He'd been hardass hell until he tore up a knee and lost a step or two. One of the best. Then he'd drifted to Atlanta and he'd done some coaching at one of the black colleges. In time we'd settled into this loose arrangement that you could call a partnership if you didn't care how you used words. The work we did the licensed PIs wouldn't touch.

And we got paid in dark money that never reached a table top.

"Beer and pork and beans," I said.

"And steak now and then, I trust," The Man said.

I nodded. A look at Hump. He tipped back his glass and poured down that smooth cognac.

"If you are short ...," The Man began.

I shook my head. "No offense, but the last time we worked for you I almost bought the farm."

"I meant … for the information."

"It didn't cost me a penny or a drop of sweat."

"Then you have my thanks," The Man said.

"I'll take an IOU for a favor when I need it."

"Agreed."

The gun near the door got our raincoats. The black opened the door and started down. I followed with Hump. As I went through the doorway and hesitated on the landing to struggle into my coat, I heard The Man say to the light-skinned gun, "Put in a call to Ben Slim in Detroit."

"You in a rush toward home?" Hump asked.

I looked at my watch. It was almost two. Marcy would be in a stone sleep by now. "A beer?"

"Something stronger," Hump said.

He picked the bar. It was one of those pretentious new places. The ones that have six months of life written on them. Free drinks to ladies from seven to nine, that kind of bar.

At two a.m. all the free-drink ladies had gone home. I ordered a Bud for myself and a double J&B on the rocks for Hump. As soon as the bartender brought the drinks and moved away Hump said, "Tell me about it."

"It's all guess." I had a swallow of the Bud. It was warm.

"Tell me a guess then."

"Atlanta's still an open city. Nobody owns it. No mob family." It was my standard five-minutes' dissertation. That the blacks owned it because they'd been there first. The girls, the drugs, the "bug" and the rest of the gambling. They owned it because they'd made the first ties. Staked the ground. Bought whatever police they needed to. And then it had changed. The Braves came in and then the Falcons and the Hawks and the Flames. That meant big-time gambling. Before the blacks knew what had happened, some whites moved in and sucked off that cream. The blacks hadn't liked it but they'd lived with it.

"And now?" Hump asked.

Another swallow of the warm beer and I tapped the bottle on the bar and got the bartender's attention. I didn't bitch. I said I'd changed my mind and I'd rather have a J&B and rocks. He brought it and I had a sip. Better.

"Somebody wants The Man's piece of it." The Man had taken it over without any trouble. He'd inherited it when Little Charlie Mako found himself on the wrong end of a butcher knife. His wife had taken the knife to him when she'd discovered that Charlie had mixed some business and pleasure with this seventeen-year-old trim. The Man had been his number-one dude and he'd moved in like the prince walks in after the king.

"Who?"

"Who wants it? Lord knows. Could be some whites, the Dixie Mafia. Could be some mob elements from out of town. Or it could be some of his own boys."

Hump sipped his J&B. "Might be a war."

"You want to soldier in it?"

"Not me, boss."

I didn't either.

It was still raining when Hump dropped me at my house. I tracked rain and mud into the living room and undressed there. The door to the bedroom was closed.

I got into bed. Marcy, still asleep, shifted to make room for me and then woke up and put an arm around my shoulders. Close up, she sniffed my breath. "That business was with a scotch bottle," she mumbled. "Hump is a bad influence."

I knew she didn't believe that. She liked Hump a hell of a lot. "That'll hurt his feelings when I tell him."

She pressed her nose against my chest and sniffed.

"No perfume?" I said.

"Not this time."

There was a time of thunder and lightning and we slept in the low hush, the falling off of the rain.

CHAPTER TWO

Hump flipped the envelope and looked at the postmark. It was ATLANTA and PM two days before. It was now Tuesday, four days after we'd made the late-night call on The Man.

All the envelope contained was a clipping from a newspaper. It had been trimmed so close it was hard to know which paper it came from.

HIT AND RUN DEATH

Local police report a man identified as Paul J. Turner of Detroit was the apparent victim of a hit-and-run driver in the early hours of Sunday morning. His body was found next to his car across the street from a tavern where he had been drinking.

Hump dropped the clipping on my coffee table. "Now we know who Ben Slim is."

"Maybe," I said.

"Maybe shit. We got that Turner dude dead."

"Indirectly." It was an act I put on for Hump. I didn't like it either."

"You shave too many words."

"It's a way of getting by," I said.

I balled up the clipping, dropped it in the ashtray and put a match to it.

It was a nothing job. A crap job. Someone had passed Benjamin Simmons on to us. It seemed he thought that his wife might be seeing another man. It could have been easier if he'd known or had some idea who the other man was. He didn't or said that he didn't.

But it was money. Fifty a day for me and fifty for Hump. Cut rates.

Wednesday, the day after the clipping arrived, we were parked on the street across from the apartment house on Piedmont. At 8:20 a.m. the husband, Simmons, came out of the apartment and got into a green LTD. When he drove past, I touched my horn, a short blast. That was to tell him we were in place, wide-eyed and curious.

It wasn't the right day. The wife, a tall blonde with a body like Miss Universe, didn't show herself until about noon. She looked about ten years younger than her husband. It was prime, in that last bloom before it begins to fall apart.

She got into her little red Porsche. We followed at a half-block distance. She led us to Lenox Square and to one of the new eating places, The Bahou Container. We gave her a two-minute lead and went in. It was easy to find her. She was seated near the front windows with another young woman.

Hump and I sat across the room from them and had beers and the king crab in the pocket of a piece of Arabic bread. They didn't seem to be in any hurry so we had a second beer and nibbled at the dish of roasted chick-peas and melon seeds that came with the drinks. When we saw that they were getting ready to leave, we beat them to the cash register and we were seated in Hump's Buick when they came out. They did a long gesturing goodbye outside the restaurant and then we tailed the Porsche to Kroger's in Ansley Mall. She was inside about twenty minutes. She came out with a big bag of groceries. Then it was straight home. We were sitting in the car at 5:20 when the husband returned. He honked at us on the way by. That meant we could go home for the night.

The next day started like a summer re-run. Simmons left for work at the proper time. We waited. And then, at 10:30 or so, she came out and got in the Porsche. She led us the back-street route to Peachtree Road. Then straight as an arrow out Peachtree, almost to Buckhead.

You could see the figure-sign about half a mile away. It was a cutout of a scuba diver with a spear gun that was bigger than he was. The sign was about ten feet high and it was on the street edge of the parking lot. The lettering on the small building identified it as the A-One Diving Equipment and School. There was a panel truck parked out front. Mrs. Simmons parked next to the panel truck and went inside. About ten minutes later she came out with a dark-haired handsome dude in a rugby shirt, white ducks and deck shoes.

They drove off in the panel truck. About seven blocks from the diving school they parked in front of a small motel. The Buck's Head Motor Hotel. We drove past and turned and came back. She'd remained in the truck while he got the key from the office. By the time we'd found a gap in the traffic so that we could make a left turn they were entering Unit #4.

Hump did a slow drive past. I wrote down the tag numbers. The pass was slow and close enough so that I could also read the sticker in the back window of the truck:

DEEP SEA DIVERS DO IT DEEPER

It was four in the afternoon when they came out of the motel room. Hump and I were across the street in the parking lot of an office building. We followed them back to the A-One Diving Equipment and School.

She didn't go inside this time. She got into the red Porsche and drove straight home. She arrived there about an hour before her husband returned from his day at work.

We met Simmons that night for a drink and the report. The meet was set up by a phone call I made. We settled upon Oliver's in Ansley Square.

I did the talking. At the end of it he was pale. He was sweating though the air-conditioning was on high. He said, "Well, I said I wanted to know and now I'm not sure."

The sweat was dripping off his chin while he wrote the check. We'd got the first hundred when we took the job. The check was for the second day. I took the check and folded it and shoved it in my pocket.

He sucked at his drink before he got his nerve up. "You two do any rough work?"

"What do you mean?"

"You know." He couldn't meet my eyes.

"Not this year."

"Maybe I shouldn't have asked," he said.

"In the circumstances I understand the question." I picked up my drink and finished it. "Think about it a day or two. Decide if it's worth it. If you still want rough work done, the man who sent you to us can probably furnish somebody to break an arm or a leg."

He nodded morosely and we left him staring down at his drink.

In the parking lot Hump hawked and spat. It wasn't that he needed to. It was the bad taste that came with the end of the job.

My phone was ringing. I could hear it from the steps while I fumbled with the door key. I got the door open and waved Hump, who was carrying a case of Bud, into the kitchen. I loped across the bedroom, picked up the receiver and sat down on the edge of the bed.

"Hello."

All I could hear was heavy breathing. I listened to it for a few seconds. One more try. "Jim Hardman here."

Still nothing but the ragged breathing.

"Look," I said, "you've got it all wrong. You're supposed to do your night breathing when a woman answers."

I thought, to hell with it, and I was pulling the receiver away from my ear when I heard a gurgle. "Hardman … this is … Billy Dawkins." Then he coughed. It sounded like it tore flesh.

"Who're you?" The name didn't mean anything to me.

"The Man's bodyguard."

"What do you want?"

"Come … over here … It's bad."

"Where?"

"You … know."

"What's wrong with you?"

"Shot," Dawkins said.

The phone rattled and banged like he was having trouble getting it back on its base. A few beats of that and the line went dead. Hump brought in two open cans of Bud. I had a swallow of mine and carried it to the closet. I got down my shoebox. The stack of money I kept stored there was getting thin. The .38 Police Positive was on top of the cash. I shoved the piece in my waistband.

Hump watched the charade without saying anything.

"The underground doctor," I said. "What's his name? He still in town?"

"Naw. He moved north."

"Know another one?"

"I know one won't ask the question," Hump said. "If that's what you mean."

"Find him. Bring him to The Man's place. I think something happened over there."

"Why they call you?"

It hadn't occurred to me. Now I shook my head. I didn't have the foggiest.

CHAPTER THREE

The first thing I saw in the back parking lot behind the auto-parts building where the man had his apartment was the black Monaco. The front windshield was shattered and the engine was still running. I leaned in long enough to turn the ignition key. On the way out, my hand touched the seatback. When I saw my hand in the dim light, there was blood on my fingers.

The entrance to the apartment was at the back of the building. The door was closed but it wasn't locked. I eased the door open and leaned in. The staircase was lighted. No one there. I took a deep breath and let it hiss out.

There was a hand smear of blood on the white wall next to the bottom step. Whoever it was had stopped there, getting it together, before he climbed the stairs. A trail of blood spots about half-dollar size led me to the landing. At the landing there'd been another stop. The close-together blood-drop design showed that. Probably he'd had to fumble for the key.

I tried the door. It was locked. I said "Shit" before I realized that the key was still in the lock. I turned it and went into the apartment.

The light-skinned black, the gun who'd been with The Man the last time we'd been there, was on the floor between the coffee table and the circular bar. He was belly down, gun in his hand, facing the door I'd just come through. He was out. Blood pooled from his left side. There was a thin blood slick under his face.

I turned him over and felt for a pulse. He was still alive. The glass from the windshield had cut his face pretty bad. There was an ugly hole low on his left side.

I left him and trotted for the kitchen. I opened a number of cabinets until I found a bundle of clean cloths. I carried half a dozen back into the living room. I squatted over him and unbuttoned his shirt. I pressed cloths over the side wound, the entry and exit holes. There wasn't much I could do about his face.

I stood and headed for the bar. I found the Hines. I poured about three shots of it into an old-fashion glass. I leaned against the bar and watched Dawkins. He didn't move.

I was looking at the bottom of the glass when I heard footsteps on the stairs. It sounded like more than one man. I picked up the .38 from where I'd put it on the bar and pointed it at the door.

"You there, Jim?" It was Hump's voice.

I yelled for him to come on in.

The black with Hump looked at least sixty years old. He wore black trousers and a blue London Fog windbreaker over a white tie shirt. He was straight-backed and moved well for his age. In one hand he carried a rolled-up paper bag.

His face threw me. At first, I thought he'd probably had the worst case of acne I'd ever seen. Then, up close, while he worked over Billy Dawkins, I saw that the scars were little crosses, tiny x's. His whole face like a fabric of x's. Later, talking to Hump, I found out that Boggs had learned all the medicine he knew in the CCC camps back in the thirties. He'd been a kid then and he'd had bad acne. A quack there, calling himself a doctor, had tried a new method, his own, that was supposed to cure it. Using a scalpel, he'd made a small cross incision on each pimple. He'd cured the acne all right but he hadn't come up with anything to do about the scars.

"How is he?"

Boggs looked up at me. "Maybe Mr. Evans told you that I'm not a real doctor?"

I said that he had.

"I can do some first aid but he needs a real doctor."

"Do the first aid."

"Mr. Evans said this one works for The Man," Boggs said.

I nodded.

"I don't want to get on the wrong side of him."

"You won't. My word on that. What do you need?"

"I could use some blankets."

I waved a hand at the bedroom. Hump went in and came back with two blankets. I sat on the sofa and watched Boggs work. He and Hump stripped Billy Dawkins to the waist. They wrapped him in the blankets except for his face and his left side, the side with the wound in it.

When there wasn't any more for Hump to do, he got the bottle of Hines and a glass and brought them to the sofa. He started to sit next to me before he remembered his manners. "Boggs, you want a drink?"

"Some straight gin."

Hump poured Boggs about a fistful of the best and passed it to him on the way by. Boggs had a long swallow of it and put the glass aside. He worked over the wound in Dawkins's side. "Cleaning it," he explained. "Got bits of cloth in it, trash like that."

He'd about finished with the wound when Dawkins groaned and moved his head. Boggs duck-walked to his paper sack and took out a needle and what looked like a vial of morphine. "Got to be careful of shock," he said. He found a vein and popped Dawkins a heavy shot.

Another swig of the gin and he bandaged the wound. He moved up a couple of feet and knelt next to the boy's face. "Not sure I'm getting all the glass out," he said. "A doctor would know more."

"You're doing fine," I said. He was. He had good hands. Gentle hands.

The door flew open and banged against the wall. The Man's other gun stood there, bent over, the two barrels of a sawed-off on us. Past him I could see The Man. He had a .45 automatic in one big fist.

"Come on in," I said. "I guess you could call us the cleanup crew."

⚜ ⚜ ⚜

Boggs packed up his paper sack and stood at the bar with one elbow bracing him. His glass was empty. I ducked under the bar opening and found the gin. I poured until he nodded. "My thanks," he said. Not only was he damned close to being a doctor but he was courtly too.

In the room beyond, the kitchen-dining room, The Man was on the phone. "Look, you can talk any kind of cheap shit you like at those civic meetings. You can talk it five days and five nights a week. Right now, I want you to get your black ass over here. And bring those solid gold instruments I've been paying for for the last five years."

He slammed down the phone. I looked at Hump. He'd heard it too. For that brief moment, those words, The Man had forgotten that he was supposed to talk like somebody out of an English drawing-room comedy.

He'd cooled some when he entered the living room and looked down at Dawkins. "How is William?"

Boggs said, "I've done as much as I can."

"This is Boggs," Hump said.

"I have heard of you. You have an excellent reputation."

"I'd said you'd pay him," Hump said.

The Man was dressed in his high fashion. He was wearing a black suit with white piping around the lapels and a white hat that might have been a planter's hat except for the wide, floppy brim. He reached in his pocket and brought out a wad of bills. From where I stood, it looked like all hundreds.

"What is your usual fee, Mr. Boggs?"

"A hundred ought to do it," Boggs said.

The Man peeled off a hundred. I edged in and reached into the wad and took that hundred and a second one. The Man looked at me with surprise.

"Of course," I said, "that fee is for office hours. This was an emergency house call." I backed away and handed the two hundreds to Boggs.

"I appreciate your help, Mr. Boggs," The Man said.

"Hump's one of my number-one men," Boggs said.

"It is the mark of a man if he attracts loyalty." The Man replaced the wad of bills. Turning, he saw the bottle of Hines. "I seem to forget that you have expensive tastes," he said to me.

"The host wasn't here. I knew he'd want me to have the best."

The Man laughed. It wasn't a real laugh. It belonged on a stage somewhere. "It bothers me," he said.

"What?"

"Why did William call you?"

I'd been worrying about that myself. So far, I hadn't come up with a guess that satisfied me. But I decided to try one and see if it fluttered in the wind. "Might be he couldn't reach you."

The Man shook his head.

Another guess floated up. It was one I didn't like. "Loyalty," I said. That nasty guess. "He was protecting you."

"I don't understand."

"Somebody caught him in the back lot. He drove right into it and it almost got him killed. He got up here but he wasn't sure that they weren't still out there."

The Man nodded. He bought that much of it.

"He knew if he called you, you might walk right into it. So, he did some hurt thinking and came up with me. A white. People out there would be looking for a black. He decided, if they were still out there, he'd offer them me. Maybe they wouldn't want me and I'd get past them."

"For the shape he was in, that was intelligent thinking."

I sat down and pulled the Hines bottle toward me. I didn't care if they saw my hand shake while I poured. "Oh shit, yes."

"How about me?" Hump had a puzzled look on his face. "I'm black."

"He did not call you," The Man said.

While they waited for the other doctor, the bodyguard who'd been with The Man, his name was Webb, took a wet mop to the stairs and wiped away most of the blood. Then he and Hump carried Billy Dawkins into the bedroom and put him on The Man's bed.

The doctor came soft-walking up the stairs. I'd seen him in the papers a few times. He was always spouting about education and causes. Now he was sweating on his cologne. He had on about three hundred dollars' worth of dark gray suit. About eighty dollars' worth of shoes and diamonds in his cufflinks.

The Man didn't do the introductions. That must have been a great relief for the doctor. The Man said, "Mr. Boggs, show him what you've done." Boggs led the doctor into the bedroom and then stepped back and closed the door behind them.

The Man picked up a thin stem of Benedictine. I hadn't even seen it poured for him. Those boys of his were fast. "You have any other educated guesses, Mr. Hardman?"

"You send me that clipping about the hit and run on P. J. Turner?"

"I had it sent."

"They got the message." I dipped my head in the direction of the bedroom. "That's the message from them."

"Tell me who these men are."

"You're not that dumb, Pike. How the hell would I know? But there are obvious possibilities. There might be others."

"Enumerate them for me," The Man said.

I looked at Hump. He flinched at *enumerate*. "Somebody wants to sit in your chair. That's not one of the possibilities. That's the reason for all this shit."

"I'm waiting patiently for the possibilities you spoke of."

"All right. One. It's somebody from outside. One of the mobs that's been tap-dancing around the city for years. Little Charlie Mako kept them out in his time and you've kept them out since him. Mafia or Dixie Mafia, you take your pick."

"I thought, perhaps, that we had convinced them that Atlanta was not healthy for them."

"Times change." I let him wait while I rolled some of the thirty-year-old cognac around on my tongue. "Two. Somebody in your own organization wants the chair. They don't want to wait for one of the natural causes. And you don't have a wife who might stick a butcher knife in you …"

"You're vague," The Man said.

"You expected me to pull a name out of the hat? Hell, the man who could have given you a name was P. J. Turner. Ben Slim could have asked him."

"Ben Slim considered it. He decided it was too dangerous to approach him."

I gave him my fun grin. "Wasn't up to it, huh?"

"Ben Slim said he'd rather kiss a rattlesnake on the mouth."

"So, he opted for the accidental hit?" I watched as The Man stepped aside. His other bodyguard, the real black one, was mopping up what was left of the blood between the coffee table and the bar. "It didn't fool anybody."

"Excuse me a moment." The Man walked into the kitchen. I could hear him dialing.

I nodded at Hump. "You had about enough of this?"

"A month's worth of it," he said.

"Georgie?" That was The Man. "Find Ray and send him to my place. I have a position for him. It might be a month or two."

"A battlefield promotion?" I said when The Man returned.

"I suppose you could call it that."

That was just talk while I finished the last of the cognac and stood and walked around the coffee table. "Do me one favor, Pike. Tell your boys the next time this happens not to call me. I'm not going to be the goat for you."

I reached the door that led to the stairs. Hump was right behind me. The Man hit the top of the bar with his open hand. It sounded like a gunshot. The black bodyguard dropped his mop in the kitchen and came at a run. He skidded to a stop next to The Man.

"You're going to work for me, Mr. Hardman."

"I don't think so," I said.

"Name your price."

"You don't have it."

Hump took one step past me and squared himself against The Man's bodyguard.

"I have anybody's price," The Man said.

"I think you know why you don't. Hump and me, we do dirty little scum jobs. This slime job and that one. But a long time ago, we decided that we wouldn't side with any part of the mob. Your side or their side or anybody's side. We work for you and we've moved off that chalk line. I won't do that and I don't think Hump will either."

"Let me put it to you this way."

"Put it any way you want to," I said. "The answer's the same."

I'd been watching Hump. I thought I was talking for him but I wasn't sure. Now he said, "He talks for me, Pike." He lifted a big

27

arm and pointed at the bodyguard. "And you, why don't you go back to your cleaning?"

"Say I passed the word here and there that you were working for me," The Man said.

"That wouldn't make it true."

"The end result would be the same. You would be in the middle. The sad part would be that you wouldn't be drawing my money and you wouldn't have my protection."

"What protection?" I took a look at the closed bedroom door to underline that and then I took a step backward and I was on the landing. Hump crossed in front of me to cover me and he caught the doorknob and jerked the door closed behind us. We clomped down the stairs. Maybe I was too angry. The mad had me. But I calmed by the time I reached the outside door, the one that led to the parking lot. I gripped the doorknob until the blood left my hand and it went numb.

"What is it, Jim?"

I think Hump thought I had my worries about what was out there in the parking lot. It wasn't that. It was the box constructed out of words. If I walked out, I'd still be his goat.

"The son of a bitch," I said. I shook my head at Hump and released the doorknob. I spun about and walked back up the stairs. The door beyond the landing was still unlocked. I pushed the door open and walked through it. Hump followed me.

The Man stood behind the bar. Two fresh glasses were on the bar counter in front of him. A fresh bottle of Hines was in his right hand. He smiled and poured two full shots.

"I thought I had overrated your intelligence," the Man said.

Hump stepped past me and picked up the two glasses. He twisted around and handed me one. His bland face to The Man, I could see that he didn't understand it yet. He didn't want to admit it in front of Pike.

I had a swallow. "Hump got it the same time I did," I said. "And he's a little pissed about it."

Hump put on his *I'm pissed* look. It would have scared Jesus.

"You stake us out like goats. You do that by passing the word we're with you. And then you watch and see who comes over and blows us away. That's not friendly."

"You have placed this in the worst possible light."

"Oh, yeah?"

Hump blinked at me. "It's scum barrel pool," he said to The Man.

"Business is like that at times," The Man said.

The choice was so limited it wasn't a choice anymore. "All right. If there's a chance we're goatmeat you're going to have to pay the goat. This is the deal. Nobody's to know we're working for you." I pointed at his bodyguard who was standing at the back of the bar, near the kitchen-dining room. "Him? What's his name?"

"Gar."

"You trust him?"

"I trust him."

I ticked them off on my fingers. "Him, the doctor, Boggs, the one that's shot. None of them knows we've been here. That's the first part of the deal."

"I can't protect you if I can't let my organization know you're working for me."

"We'll take our chances."

He nodded. "We have an agreement."

"A thousand dollars a week until it's over. At the end, if we've turned up the name or names, another five thousand to each of us to close it out."

"That is a lot of money."

"Your problem," I said.

"Do you know how many quarters have to be collected on the bug to add up to your fee?"

I didn't feel like doing the math. "Screw all that," I said. "It's a business expense."

CHAPTER FOUR

"Muddy dark," Hump said.

I looked up at the sky and then realized he wasn't talking about natural matters. He was doing a metaphor on me. I decided to do one back at him.

"It's like being blindfolded in a cow pasture." That was a rural metaphor. It had to do with not knowing exactly what you were stepping on. Hump was a city boy. I wasn't sure he'd ever been in a cow pasture.

But I had a list in my head. Getting it out of The Man had been like asking him to pay taxes on the income from the drug trade. He hadn't wanted to. He'd said I didn't need those names. I'd blown up at him. "If I don't have the names how the hell am I supposed to check on them?"

He'd folded. He'd written the list for me. Four names. The structure of his outfit. The four men in his organization with enough power to go after his chair. And enough ambition. When you had enough ambition to head one of the units you had enough to run for President.

Smiley Gibbs. Girls.
Bobby Biddoux. The Bug.
Jack Tyrone. Other gambling.
Flash Timmers. Drugs.

I'd read the list three or four times. Then I sipped the Hines and closed my eyes and repeated them to myself. One more look and I passed the list back to The Man. He burned the list with a flick of his gold lighter.

I stopped next to my Ford. It was a clear, bright night. A spill of stars as far as I could see. That wouldn't change. Closer, in the parking lot, the black Monaco with the shattered windshield was gone. It had been towed away while we'd been inside.

Hump trailed me and stood digging a toe in the gravel layer that coated the lot. "This might take a year."

"Then we'll get rich. You want to pick one?"

"Smiley Gibbs."

I laughed at him. "That figures. The girls."

"It was your question."

That was true. "First thing in the morning…"

Hump shook his head. "He'd be sleeping. Smiley's got an upside-down life. I'll look for him tonight."

"Easy," I said.

"All my dumb brothers are dead."

I opened the car door and got inside. "Check in with me."

"Tomorrow afternoon."

He left. I started up the Ford and backed it around. My headlights lit the back door of The Man's building. The doctor, coming out, whirled and put his face against the door. He was a shy one all right. He remained that way until I swung the Ford toward the driveway and the lights left him.

"I'm coming by," Art Maloney said.

Art's still on the force. We'd been friends there and he'd had to back away for a few months after the way I left a step or two ahead of an inquiry. The years passed and that eased some and he's one of the two or three people I trust.

It was eight in the morning by the clock on the night table. I'd slept well. I hadn't even groaned when the phone rang.

"Why?"

"A couple of people want to talk to you. I think I'm supposed to do the introductions."

I swung my feet over the side of the bed and sat up. "That necessary? They shy?"

He ignored the *shy* remark. "They think so."

I had a shower and dressed. I carried my shoes and socks into the kitchen and put on enough water to make a single cup of instant. I had my shoes on by the time the water boiled. I made myself a cup and filled the kettle. I went outside and found the *Constitution* under a bush where the paper boy had tossed it. I was reading the sports page when the doorbell rang.

I opened the door and waved the three of them in. Art had a big bakery bag with him. He tossed the bag to me. "I brought the Sticky Buns."

"Coffee water's hot."

I didn't look at the two men with Art until they were seated at the kitchen table. I was at the stove making the instant. Art tore open the bakery bag and passed around a handful of napkins.

The men were about the same size. Big, heavy-shouldered studs. Dressed better than Art. Not as shabby. Maybe they didn't have as many kids as Art did.

"Baylor," Art said. He pointed at the one with the weathered face and the dark hair with the gray cowlick.

Baylor took a bite of the Sticky Bun and did a quarter of an inch of a nod.

"Franklin." That one had deep creases in his face like knife scars. Brown hair that he probably dyed.

I passed the cups of instant to Art and he handed them around. I dropped some spoons in the center of the table and placed the milk carton next to Art. I eased into a chair and pulled

THE LAST OF THE ARMAGEDDON WARS

the bakery bag toward me. I broke off a bun and had my first bite. Usually if the bun were made right the dark syrup had pecans stuck in it. These looked like they had a half-and-half mixture of pecans and cashews.

"Thanks for seeing us." That was Baylor, the one with the weathered face and the gray cowlick.

I heard the hoarse voice and tabbed it. "Face-to-face this time instead of on the phone?"

Baylor looked at Art. I think there was an accusation on the front of his tongue. Art had a wedge of bun in his mouth. He chewed slowly while he shook his head. After a swallow he said, "I told you he wasn't dumb."

"No harm done," Baylor said. "Now he knows how we know. We can walk past all the early crap."

Art muffled a yawn. "Anything that saves times."

"The way we figure it, we made you a bundle," Franklin said. "The info must have been worth a grand."

"If you passed it," Baylor said.

I'd been watching their faces and tasting their attitudes. They did sound right. They didn't seem to have the right amount of nasty in them, what I usually got from guys on the force who knew about my time there and how I'd left.

"If the phone line's not down between here and Detroit you know I passed it."

"P. J. Turner? Yeah, we heard about that." Baylor had a sip of the coffee. He pulled the milk carton toward him and tipped in a couple of tablespoons.

"I'd better correct one misunderstanding," I said. "It was free from you and free from me. I didn't put in a bill."

"That doesn't sound like you," Franklin said.

Baylor grunted. "Maybe you'll collect some other way."

Now it had shifted. What I'd expected of them. I took a couple of bites of Sticky Bun and chewed. Screw them. It was their visit and their need to talk. I'd wait them out until suppertime if

I had to. This went on much longer and I'd get a deck of cards and practice dealing seconds. That would amuse them.

"Jim." Art worried his tongue at a piece of nut caught in his teeth. "These two don't really know you."

"That's true." Dry as dust.

"All they've got to go on are those stories they've heard about you. How much you like money. That kind of thing."

"They offering me money?"

Art laughed. "Not directly."

"That's the way I like it best. Directly."

"What they want is a favor." Art had done his part. He'd built the bridge.

Baylor leaned forward. "The information we gave you. That should have put you in tight with Pike."

"As tight as any cracker gets with him," I said.

Art pushed back his chair. He filled the kettle at the sink and put it over the burner. He braced a hip against the kitchen counter and stood over us. If he had to he'd referee.

Franklin wanted in. "But you've worked for him before and he trusts you?"

"As much as he trusts anybody. Right up to the moment when you turn the corner and go out of sight. That's when it stops."

"But you can get close?"

"If I wanted to."

"Come on, Hardman. Damnit, there's a war about to start."

I said, "It's already started."

At the end of my telling it, the water in the kettle was whistling. Art passed the jar of instant coffee and then he followed it, pouring in the water.

Baylor gave his cup an easy stir and dropped the spoon on the table. "Any report of a shooting in that area last night?"

Art shrugged. "It wasn't cold last night but you can bet the windows were closed. If anybody made the mistake of hearing any shooting, they went deaf as of yesterday."

"That's another one he owes you," Franklin said.

"A small one."

"How do you see it, Jim?" Art pulled the bakery bag toward him and broke off one of the last three buns.

"The same way you do. A payback. You hit my hitman and I blow away one of yours."

"It's even now," Baylor said.

"You believe that?"

"Don't you?"

"Only when pigs take off and land on aircraft carriers."

Art agreed. "It's round one and this could last fifty rounds."

"You two are from Intelligence. You tell me who wants to hit Pike and why."

"I knew that," Baylor said, "and I'd run for God."

"And you'd get my vote." I broke off the next to the last bun and tore off a big chunk.

"Until we know you're our key to Pike's door," Franklin said.

"It's a cardboard key." I said it with my mouth full. Even to me it sounded like I was talking under water. "And if you think I'm going to play informer for you, you can get the fuck out of my house."

It shocked them. It was too calm, too reasonable.

"Informer's a bad word," Baylor said.

"Fink, snitch, stoolie?"

I waited. He didn't seem to be very fast. He couldn't come up with a word that made you feel you were doing it for God and country and Mom.

"Spy, secret agent?" I added those just to corner the rest of the market. There wasn't much left for him.

Baylor gave it up. "You want a gang war here in Atlanta?"

"It's no red off my candy." I turned and faced Art. "I was right, wasn't I? These two are from Intelligence?"

Art nodded.

"Then why the fuck don't they go be intelligent somewhere? They've got my phone number. They proved that. Now all they've got to do is find out what's going on and they call me and I call Pike."

"It's not that easy. Even if it was, we need to know from the inside what Pike is going to do."

"You really want to know?" I eased that in softly.

"Sure."

Sucked him in. "I can tell you that now. Somebody wants his turf. What the hell you think he's going to do? You think he got the throne and holds it by being dumb and gutless?"

"A fight?"

"A mean one. Birdwatchers that go trampling through the woods are going to be tripping over bodies for a fucking year."

"I don't want that to happen," Baylor said. "You've got the key."

"Like I've been telling you, it's cardboard. The first rain and it falls apart."

Baylor looked at Art. "You know what he's talking about?"

"It's a metaphor," Art said.

Old Art. Good old Art. We'd taken those classes together at Georgia State and he'd remembered some of it. I guess he'd only been sleeping half the time.

"That is, if he's the key, then he's a weak one."

"All we want is information."

"No way," I said. "I work for you one time and you own me. You can hold that over my head for the rest of my life."

Baylor pushed his empty cup toward the center of the table. He stood. "You still making trips to New York?"

"Not for a couple of years."

"Still doing favors for cash without a license?"

I didn't answer that one.

"What I'm saying is that if you put your back to us it is going to be hard for you to do much of anything."

"Maybe I can get welfare."

Baylor and Franklin headed for the living room. I followed them as far as the kitchen doorway. Behind me, Art hadn't moved from his place at the table. A look over my shoulder and I saw him sneak-grab the last bun.

Baylor opened the front door. Franklin stepped through. I thought Baylor had finished. He hadn't. "Remember, Hardman. You've been warned. A building's going to fall on you."

I didn't look at Art while I straightened up the kitchen. The used cups in the sink, the bag and the wrapping paper from the buns in the trash. The milk in the refrigerator. That done, I made myself a fresh cup and sat down across from him.

"That your idea?"

"What?" The bland, the innocent look.

"That whipsaw."

"Oh, that?"

"That," I said.

"I told them you wouldn't buy it."

"That makes all the difference in the world. That restores my faith in mankind."

"Look," Art said, "I couldn't shortstop it. The word was from pretty far up."

"How far up?"

"How far is really up?" Art said.

"That high?"

"All I know is those two came to me. Said they needed a talk with you. Asked me to set it up. I wanted to know why. They told me. I said I wouldn't do it. And I said I didn't want to do it either. They told me I'd better. I put in a call to the Captain while they waited. He said he'd call me back. A couple of minutes later he called back and he said I'd better do it. I said that was horseshit.

He said it might be but it was horseshit from pretty high, close to heaven."

"Curious," I said.

"More than that," Art said. He waved a hand at the front door. "As soon as those two get back downtown, as soon as they pass the word about the shooting at The Man's place, the pressure is going to rattle the walls."

"It's time I took a vacation." I sipped my coffee and winked at him.

"That would be good sense."

"The mountains or the beach?"

"Either," he said.

Art left a few minutes later. He was tired after his night shift. I gave him a minute and then went into the bedroom and dialed Hump's home number. He didn't answer.

CHAPTER FIVE

When there wasn't an answer at Hump's apartment by noon, I checked a few of the lunch or late-breakfast cafés that Hump liked. That was a hopeful assumption. There was always the chance he was still in some girl's bed. A lot of beds in town had developed a six-six or -seven trough down one side of the mattress.

My fifth stop was Pig's Place. That's a barbecue joint out on Auburn. I think it's an all-night café. If it closes at all it's for five minutes while they throw the drunks out and empty the ashtrays.

This part of Auburn used to be the center of the black world in Atlanta. It's changed now. It's dying on the integration vine. The movie houses closed down the street when it got so blacks could move out of the balcony at the Rialto. Barber shops, pool halls and restaurants died in the same street-life emigration.

Shuttered and boarded buildings, eyesore here and there. Empty lots grow the town's best weeds. The corner boys have all combed their afros and caught the bus that drops them at the corner of Luckie and Forsyth.

The block with Pig's Place on it still has some rank breath left. The barber shop's open a few doors south and the pool hall has its trash bags on the curb and that must mean some of the shooters are still around.

From a block or two away, if your car window's down, you can smell the sweet-grease scent from the pits in back of Pig's Place. If you're born south, it starts your mouth watering. If you're from the north or the west you might wonder why it's always pork and never beef. Ask that question and you won't get an answer. Nobody even understands the question.

The lettering in the window gives you the real name of the café. Pig's Barbecue Emporium. That's *long* for the real name. Inside, past the patched screen door, there's a bar-like counter that takes up most of the right side of the place. The rest of the long room is a scatter design of small tables covered with red-and-white oilcloth tablecloths. If the barbecue smell didn't overpower it, you'd be able to smell the oilcloth.

By ten after one, the early lunch crowd had left. There were a couple of dudes at the counter eating the rib sandwich special. They were cutting the grease with tall cans of Colt 45 Malt.

There were four or five occupied tables at the rear of the café. All blacks. I was the only white. Not only in the cafe but probably on the whole block.

I passed the two dudes at the counter and stop. I waited until the counterman eased a clean damp cloth in my direction, a sweeping, circular motion, and gave me a mock surprised look.

"You want something to take out?"

"Hump Evans around?"

"He's fuzz," one of the dudes at the bar said.

"No," I said, "I'm Jim Hardman."

"Hardman?" The counterman sucked air through his teeth. "You run with Hump some?"

"Some."

"I still say he's fuzz," the dude said.

I shook my head. The headshake was for the counterman. I wasn't up for any kind of discussion with the dude at the counter.

The counterman stopping sucking air. He lifted an arm and pointed at the back, kitchen door. "He's back there. At the pits."

I nodded and headed in that direction. I'd gone about three steps when I heard the same black dude push at it one more time. "I still say he's fuzz and …"

"Shut it up," the counterman said. "Hump Evans will come down on your head."

"On whose head? He come down on me and ..."

"Mouth can get ass in trouble," the counterman said. "And ass can't even ask why."

Past the door, I was in a kitchen. A shrunken little man stood over a bank of kitchen ranges. He was drinking iced tea from a huge glass. He saw me and his head jerked up.

"Hump Evans?"

"Out there." He dropped his head again. On the way by, I saw that he was stewing fresh corn in a small skillet.

Outside the barbecue smell was stronger. Apart from the café building, separated by a breezeway, was a covered shed. The pits were there and there was a stainless-steel table. It was about as big as a pool table and there was about seventy or eighty pounds of whole pig on it. The pig was just off one of the pits and he'd been flattened out, legs straight out. Put a string on that pig and you could have flown him as a kite.

Hump was facing me across the table. He lifted his head and said, "You looking for me?"

"It's afternoon."

The black working the pit had his back to me. Now he turned and I got a look at the x-marked scars on his face. It was the underground doctor from the night before at The Man's.

"You remember Boggs?" Hump said.

"Sure." I nodded at him. He nodded back and flashed me a grin.

Hump had a beer bottle in each hand. One was half full and the other full. "Have my spare, Jim."

I took it and had my first swallow for the day. I edged around and stood at the end of the table. "What's going on?"

"I'm watching the surgeon at work."

Boggs laughed. It was a free, easy laugh. I think I understood it then. Why Hump was one of his good men. Hump saw him without the scars. That was important. I wished I could too. All I saw was that dumbass CCC quack.

We watched while Boggs cut away the hams and the shoulders. He put those aside. Hump leaned in and, getting Bogg's nod, stripped away a peel of the lean. It was crisp and dark. Hump broke the peel down the middle and passed half of it to me. We looked at each other and chewed.

"Damned good," I said. "The best."

"It might not be my best," Boggs said. "I think I let my vinegar hand shake while I was making the sauce."

"Live with it," Hump said. "And quit all that being modest."

Boggs grinned and nodded. "You were thinking about the ribs, Mr. Evans?"

"Do me a plate of rib surgery," Hump said. He licked his fingers and smiled at me. "Had your lunch yet?"

"Been too busy hunting you."

"Make that two plates of rib surgery, Mr. Boggs."

"Yes, Mr. Evans."

"And stop that mister shit."

Bogg's laugh followed us through the kitchen. We passed up the back tables. Hump picked one near the front, toward the wall, some distance from the bar counter. He waved me to a chair. Walking, he had the last foam swallow from his beer bottle. He placed the bottle on the counter and waited. The two black dudes were still at the bar, two or three bar stools off to Hump's right.

"Another one, Hump?"

"The first one went down," Hump said.

The counterman popped the cap from a bottle and placed it in front of Hump. He kept his hand on it when Hump reached for it. The counterman's head was turned and he was staring at the black who'd insisted I was fuzz. "You got something to say to Mr. Evans, Willie?"

"Me?" Willie lifted his head from his plate, all the innocent surprise in the world on his face. "I hardly know the gentleman."

The counterman giggled. He drew his hand away from Hump's beer. He leaned away. "That's what I thought, Willie."

Hump had a puzzled look on his face when he sat down across the table from me. "What was that about?"

"Black is beautiful, white is ugly."

"Huh?"

"Willie didn't believe you knew any whites," I said.

"Willie don't look much too beautiful to me," Hump said. He said it loud enough. Willie didn't move.

Boggs brought in our plates with a high-class waiter's flourish. The plates were piled high with ribs. He placed them in front of us with a wink and returned to the kitchen. He returned a few seconds later with a bowl of cole slaw and a dish of stewed corn. The slaw smelled like his vinegar hand had shook again.

Boggs leaned close. "Next is the surprise. Had to twist the cook's arm."

"Thank you, Doctor."

"You aint' seen it yet," Boggs said.

"Got to trust the doctor," Hump said.

We were working on the ribs when Boggs returned. He carried a huge plate. On it was the biggest skillet-sized hoecake I'd ever seen. I don't think Hump knew exactly what it was, but I could see the dark specks and pieces in it.

"Jesus," I said, "cracklin bread."

Boggs flashed his grin. He went away happy. Another time or two and I think I'd be one of his men too.

Hump passed the bottle that was in the center of the table, next to the salt and pepper. It was full of some pale brown liquid. Chunks of red pepper floated in it. "That's the fire hot."

I went easy on it. It was fire hot. I worked over the ribs and the slaw and the cracklin bread. I waited until he'd slowed down on his ribs. "I thought you were supposed to call me."

"It was a long night." Hump sprinkled the fire hot on some ribs. "You know what night it turned out to be?"

I shook my head.

"It was the May dance."

"What's that?"

"I was looking for Smiley Gibbs."

I knew that. Smiley was on the list. He ran the girls for The Man.

"Found him at The Player's Supper Club. It turned out it was the big night of the year. They were picking the Pimp of the Year."

I'd heard about that once. It sounded like fun.

"Tell me about it."

Lordy, lordy, lordy, those dudes were dressed. That nature thing about the males being the ones with the bright feathers. Man, you should have seen these dudes. Velvet jumpsuits. Dinner jackets with satin lapels. White silk suits with gold buttons.

And the flock of foxes. He'd never seen such girls. Black and tan and cream and white. All shades and colors and all sizes.

The doorman didn't want to let Hump in. He stood there in the doorway and watched the pimps and the foxes passing by, going in. The doorman was about as big as Hump. Six-four or -five and two-thirty or so.

"The Club is closed tonight."

"It don't look closed to me," Hump said.

"It's a private party. By invitation only."

"It might be I know somebody in there."

"You're not a player?" It was an assessment.

Hump shook his head. "Might be I know one."

"He got a name?"

"Johnny Cott might know me."

The doorman leaned inside and waved. A skinny black kid with a high afro came out. "You know Mr. Johnny Cott?"

The kid said he did.

"See if you can find him."

The kid hurried away. Hump backed out of the traffic. He stood shoulder-to-shoulder with the doorman. The pimps carried their invitations in white-gloved hands. The doorman knew most of them. He checked about one in five.

One of the pimps looked at Hump. "You grow a shadow tonight, Bill."

The doorman smiled. "It looks that way."

After the pimp went in, the doorman looked Hump up and down. "I know you?"

"Hump Evans."

"Played some ball?"

"Some," Hump said.

"Browns."

"That was the one."

"I never got past the taxi squad," the doorman said. "That was back when they had them."

"Where?"

"Name the team and I was there," the doorman said. "Pittsburgh two years, a year with Miami, two years with the Falcons."

"I didn't get your name."

"Bill Cinch."

"Grambling?"

Cinch nodded.

"Left tackle? Saw you play. Good pass rush, trouble with the run." It was an honest estimate. No reason for lying.

"That was it. The rush ran me right out of the league."

The kid returned. "I can't find Cott. He ain't here yet."

Cinch waved him away. "You know Cott?"

"I know him."

"Go on in, Hump. One more won't matter. Cott comes and I'll tell him you're at the bar."

"Appreciate it." Hump gave his necktie a twist. "Have a drink with me later."

"Might be," Cinch said.

It was tacky-decoration night, too. Or maybe it was just somebody's idea of funky. The huge barroom was dressed out like the set for a junior-senior dance in one of those 1940s movies. Colored crepe-paper streamers, clusters of balloons and party favors at each table.

God, Hump thought, somebody has missed their childhood. They spent it in reform school.

But the booze was real. The sign over the bar worried him: ALL DRINKS $1.00. After Hump pushed his way to the bar and ordered a scotch he carried it away and had a slow sip. No, it was the real thing. It wasn't the bar brands. J&B or better. Now that was the way to run a party.

He had his slow look around the room. Once you got past the high-school decorations, it was a glare of white. All the tables were covered with starched white tablecloths. In the center of each table was a name card in a holder. Most of the tables were taken. Each table with its pimp and his flock. From two to five women a table. Bright feathers on all of them. The pimp in his best, the finest that tricking and young flesh could buy. The foxes all curled and polished. Oh, it was a glitter of a thing.

"Voted yet?"

A lean, dark man in a tux stood next to Hump. He held a thick stack of cards in one hand.

"No."

The man passed him a card and a pen.

PIMP OF THE YEAR

May 7, 1976

———————————

(one name only)

Hump printed in the only one he knew well. *Johnny Cott.* He returned the card and the pen to the man in the tux. The man placed the card on the bottom of the stack without looking at it and moved away.

His first drink was gone. Hump shoved his way to the bar for a second. When he turned, he bumped into Johnny Cott.

"Hey, there."

"I been looking for you," Cott said. "Cinch said you'd lied your way in here. Told him all your girls were off taking a drunk cure."

"Cinch said that?"

"Of course."

Cott was about six-one. Lean. Just on the other side, the far side, of handsome. Hair straightened and slicked down like some Latin lover in silent flicks. A flowerlike scar ruined his right cheek. It looked like it might have been made with a beer-can opener. Girls used to carry them around in their pockets when Hump had been a corner boy.

"I just voted for you," Hump said.

"Then I got two votes. Your vote and mine. Now I got to win." He caught Hump by the elbow and steered him down the aisle between the tables. "Might be you'll bring me luck. I got this spare chair at my table. One of my prime has got a virus."

"I do that," Hump said, "and I might get a few votes myself."

"Foxes don't vote," Cott said.

"Nothing wrong with getting a zero the first time you run," Hump said. And then they were at Cott's table. There were three girls seated there. He knew the older one. A woman and not a girl. A shade past thirty, tall and starting to put on weight around the hips. That was Mabel. She'd been Johnny Cott's first girl, the one he'd turned out and bought walking shoes. That had been over ten years ago and it was as close as a marriage except when Johnny needed some cash.

Hump leaned over Mabel and kissed her on her cheek. "I know this beauty." Closer, whispering, he said, "You still the main woman for this slick?"

That got a smile. "The only one."

"No whispering," Cott said. He sat in the chair on Mabel's left. "People see that they might think you're jumping my fences. They think that and I might have to cut you." He flicked his empty hand about, a parody of a knife fight. "Sit your big self down, Hump."

Hump took the empty chair. He was seated between two young girls.

"Girl on your left is Zelda."

Zelda smiled at Hump. Even, though pointed, teeth. About five-two barefooted. Low-cut white gown. A straight down hang of pearls that buried themselves in the space between her breasts. Handful breasts.

"On your right is Effi."

A tall, slat-lean girl. Tennis-ball breasts. No bra. Her black hair cut short and close, flapper style out of the 1920s. Impish face. Her eyes read him right down to his underwear.

Both girls had their looks at Hump. Then both turned to Johnny Cott. "He's not a player," Cott explained. That should have been enough but it wasn't. *All right, he's not a pimp. What is he?* "As far as I know, Mr. Hump Evans don't do anything for a living. But he's always got a money roll. Must be an inheritance."

"Income from a trust," Hump said.

At the stand at the back of the room a five-piece band had come back from a break. It was gut music, thumping and humping music. The tall girl, Effi, got in the first grab.

"You dance, Hump?"

Hump waited. Eyes on Johnny Cott. "Mind if we dance?"

"Tonight's free. Call it a holiday. For a friend anyway." Cott leaned across the table, "But if you run off with one of my girls, she better show up tomorrow ready for the night's work."

"If those are the rules…"

"Those are the rules," Cott said.

Hump did his gentleman. When he pulled back Effi's chair he saw, past her, the pout on Zelda's face. That is all right, little girl, he was saying to her. It is a long time between now and the end of this party. There is some time for you yet.

And then he and Effi were on the dance floor. No room to move. Hipped and shouldered on all sides. All those bodies and all that perfume and men's cologne. Heady stuff. They were dancing close. Her head, the top of it, against his chin. Some part of her moving against his groin. Light ruffling. Might be a hand.

"Oooh," she said, batting her eyes at him.

"If I lied," Hump said, "I'd say that wasn't half of it."

The music ended. It was just in time, Hump decided, to keep him from making a fool of himself. He walked Effi back to the table. The gentleman again with the chair. He stood behind her and looked over at Cott. "I'm dry. I get you anything from the bar?"

Cott pushed back his chair. "I'll walk with you."

At the fringe of the bar, waiting his time, Hump said, "I think I'm in the wrong business."

Cott grinned. "It's got its minutes now and then."

Hump edged to the bar. Rum-and-tonics for the girls and scotch-and-rocks for him and Cott. He passed two of the drinks to Cott and carried the other three. "Smiley Gibbs here?"

"You know Smiley?" Cott turned in the aisle, blocking it.

"Not sure," Hump said. "Think I met him this one time."

"He's here. Wouldn't miss it." Hands full, Cott nodded toward the bandstand. "Front table. One on the far right. Closest to the restrooms." He leaned close and grinned. "Had his choice. Could have been next to the kitchen or the restroom. Took the restrooms. Seems he's got a weak bladder."

Hump had his look. Two men and one woman at the table. One man was bulldog-faced, short and thick-chested.

Bitter-chocolate dark. Gray in his hair. The other man with him had the flunky look. Suit might have been from Sears. Bulge under his arm. Probably Smiley Gibbs's gun. The woman with Gibbs was light as white.

"Short one?"

"That's him," Cott said. "He's got the power to move you to Backwoods, Alabama, he wants to."

"How?"

"He tells you. He's all grease and friendly. He says something about how good Backwoods, Alabama, is this time of year. Then you go home and pack your suitcase."

"And if you don't?"

"They break some important parts of you," Cott said.

They reached the table. They passed the drinks around. Hump sat between Effi and Zelda. Zelda said, in a mock whisper, "You've been mean to me," and put a slim hand on Hump's leg.

Cott checked his watch. "It's time."

On the bandstand the members of the band got the signal and did a ragged fanfare. The dance floor emptied. Hump faced Zelda and said, "You're going to be sorry you keep that up."

Zelda laughed. Hump could see her tonsils.

At the front table, Smiley Gibbs was standing. He had a sheet of paper in one hand. The tabulations, Hump figured.

"I'm not the kind to be sorry," Zelda said.

Smiley Gibbs reached the steps that led, from the right side, up to the bandstand. His bodyguard, grinning, carried a huge, ugly monster of a trophy. It had a gold gleam to it and, from what Hump could see from that distance, it might have been in the shape of a standing nude woman.

The band leader fumbled with the mike. He was lowering it so that it would be at the right level for Gibbs. Gibbs and his bodyguard were two steps away from the mike when the kitchen door whammed open and three men entered at a crouched run. All three wore stocking masks and carried sawed-off shotguns.

A woman screamed. About fifty more joined in.

Gibbs's bodyguard dropped the trophy and got a hand into his jacket. That was as far as he got before the first shotgun blast cut him down. Part of that same blast hit Smiley Gibbs and knocked him on his butt.

Across the table from Hump, Johnny Cott put an arm around Mabel's shoulders and pushed or pulled her to the floor. That left Hump with two girls. He pushed Zelda over backward and grabbed Effi. Just before Hump ducked below the level of the table, he saw one of the other shotgun men step to the center of the bandstand and fire both barrels into Smiley Gibbs.

One of the shotgun men hadn't fired. He covered the kitchen doorway while the other two made their run for the kitchen. Then he ducked away and followed. Nobody moved after them.

Then Hump was under the table facing Johnny Cott. Eyeball to eyeball, smelling each other's scared sweat.

Johnny Cott said, "Now I'll never know if I won."

CHAPTER SIX

I looked down at my plate. There were still a couple of ribs that I hadn't touched. I couldn't handle them. The cracklin bread and the stewed fresh corn had done me in. I felt packed hard in places I'd never been packed before. "You eat other people's lunch, Hump?"

"That's how I got my full growth." Hump reached across the table and got the rib cluster. He dropped it on a bare spot on his plate.

"And after that?"

"After what?" Hump eyed my plate. There wasn't anything left on it but bones and crumbs.

"After Smiley Gibbs got scratched off our list."

"Oh, that." He lifted a rib and held it like an ear of corn, turning it as his teeth tore at it. "Everybody suddenly decided there were better places to be. That the band wasn't funky enough. That the election had probably been rigged anyway."

"Huh?" I had a swallow of beer and felt it hit the hard packing and almost bounce back.

"What all that means is that those dudes and their ladies left in such a hurry they widened the front and the back doors."

"And you?"

"I looked at the trophy. It was kind of dented some."

"And?"

"Then I took Effi home and protected her the rest of the night." He looked at his watch. "Until about two hours ago."

"With your body?"

"Of course." He laughed. "Kept my body between her and all those stray bullets."

"Poor Zelda," I said.

"That pretty child wasn't pushy enough. I hope she learned her lesson."

"A few things bother me."

"Name them." Hump waved two fingers at the bartender. More beer.

"There wasn't anything in the paper this morning."

"Don't expect it to be in the afternoon either," Hump said. "I have a feeling that Smiley Gibbs and his bodyguard just left town on an extended vacation."

The bartender brought us the two beers. While he was collecting the empties, I could see that his head was doing the math on the lunch tab.

"Stewed corn ain't on the menu," he said. He lifted a crust of the cracklin bread, looked at it with almost a comic intensity, and then popped it in his mouth and chewed. "Cracklin bread ain't either."

"What stewed corn?" Hump said. "What cracklin bread?"

The bartender left shaking his head.

"And nobody called the police?" I pulled my fresh beer toward me and had a small sip.

"That bunch? Those dudes there last night, not one of them even knows that nasty number."

"What else worries me is that I haven't heard from The Man."

"I called him," Hump said.

"That right?"

"He'd already heard. I must have been call number two hundred and twenty-seven."

"He upset?"

"Some."

"On a scale of one to ten."

"Let me put it this way. He asked me why I didn't go up there and kick the shit out of those three men with the shotguns. He said that he had hired me. I told him that I had gone up there to the bandstand and kicked the shit out of at least two of them and that was why I was bleeding into the telephone."

"Funny," I said.

"He didn't think so. At least he didn't do any laughing."

"Nobody ever accused him of having a sense of humor."

"That secret its safe with me," Hump said.

"Last part that bothers me. How the hell was I supposed to find out about this? I mean, it is important."

"I said I'd tell you."

"Just when was that going to happen?"

"Now," Hump said. "Right now."

I gave up. I leaned back in my chair and sipped my beer and belched quietly a few times. Hump did his slow walk through what was left of the lunch.

At the end we flipped for the whole bill. Stewed corn and cracklin bread included. He lost.

"Local talent? Imported talent?"

"All three were black," I said. "Hump neglected to get their Social Security numbers."

It was an hour or so later. Hump and I had split outside of Pig's Place. He'd gone to his apartment for a shave and a shower and a change of clothes. I'd driven home, the heartburn beginning to creep up on me.

I walked around my phone for about fifteen minutes. I had to get past some reservations I had about making the call.

I reached Baylor at home. I made a speech. I made it hard-assed strong. I wasn't playing fink for him. I was trading information. Mine for his. That was the way it was or it wasn't going to be any way at all.

He gave me his Cub Scout oath and I told him about the killing of Smiley Gibbs.

"Crazy way to do it, don't you think?"

I said I thought there were some question marks about style and good sense.

"Showy," Baylor said. "If they want a good clean hit it's about the bottom of all the possible ways to handle it."

"Rock bottom," I agreed.

"You want to hit Gibbs, you do it in a flyby in the parking lot. You do it in the dark on his doorstep. What you don't do is pull it right in front of two or three hundred people."

"Unless...?"

"Unless it is show-and-tell time."

"The Western Union message killing?"

"That's the way I see it." Baylor coughed and cleared his throat. Somebody is saying that there ain't no way the in-power organization, The Man, can protect them anymore. He can't even protect his man, Gibbs."

"Erosion?"

"A lot of people peed in their pants last night."

"With good reason," I said.

And then he'd asked if it was local talent or imported.

And I'd given him my snot answer.

"A team? Three men." A pause. "I'll ask around."

"Remember."

"What?"

"This is a two-way street. What I know for what you know. Don't short me."

"That was the deal." Baylor sounded distant, like I'd hurt his feelings. "And to show good faith, I'll try to do a bonus this time."

"What?"

"Wait and see."

I said I would and broke the connection.

I didn't like it. I didn't like it one bit. I'd lost my cherry and hadn't got a thing for it. Baylor and Franklin, that mothering bunch. I didn't watch out I'd get caught in the middle. Or they'd get something strong and rank on me and own me.

Cops. I'd been one myself. I knew. Once they owned your balls you might as well give them the rest of the body. Bald head to untrimmed toenails.

I'd opened a beer in the kitchen. I carried it into my backyard. I sat on the back steps and looked at the green fog of May as far as I could see. Far off in the distance, past some backyards, I could see a clump of dogwoods. The bloom and cluster like snow. I was half dozing, thinking of snow and other climates, when I heard Hump pull into my drive. I waited until he cut his engine. Then I whistled. He heard me and walked around the side of the house. He was carrying a road Bud with him. He sat down on the step next to me.

"I was going to call but your phone was busy."

I nodded. I wasn't sure I was ready to tell Hump about that Police Intelligence tie-up yet. I'd have to. Not yet.

"Had this call when I was in the shower."

"Effi wants a rerun?"

"Remember me telling you about Bill Cinch?"

I didn't. I shook my head.

"The guy who'd played at Grambling and had been on some pro taxi squads?"

"The doorman," I said.

"He's shaky now but I think he knows something."

"Why you? Lot of numbers in the Atlanta phonebook."

"I think he'd heard I'd done some work for The Man."

"And…?"

"Like I said, he's shaky. He doesn't want to talk to The Man. He wants to talk through somebody."

"You," I said.

"And you, too, on my word."

I stood up and carried my empty to the big green garbage cart the city had furnished everybody a few months back. I lifted the top, got a whiff of last week, and dropped my can in. "When?"

"Now."

"He tell you what it's about?"

"I've got my guess," Hump said.

I had mine too. It was too easy. I didn't trust easy much. "You trust him?"

"I just met the dude."

I didn't have to say it. Hump knew it as well as I did. It could be a box. A setup. It hadn't been long. Maybe it didn't take long. If the word was out that Hump and I were working for The Man, there were some damned good reasons to be wary.

I left Hump on the back steps. I went into the bedroom and reached up in my closet and got down the shoe box. I lifted out the .38 P.P. and put in fresh loads. I got a hand towel from the bathroom and wrapped the piece in it. I carried it down the steps and stood and watched while Hump finished his roady.

Then we got into Hump's Buick. I placed the towel-wrapped piece on the seat next to my right leg. Wedged there.

We went to meet Bill Cinch.

Hump cruised the Bedford-Pines redevelopment areā. Now that the warm weather was coming there were some signs that the contractors had thawed out. It was a matter of some run-down apartment houses, ones with the windows broken and the doors kicked in. Work crews were ripping away the insides of the apartment houses and leaving only the shells. By the end of the summer the apartments were supposed to be ready for black families to move in. I didn't think they'd make it.

It was a slow loop Hump drove. Especially slow. It got us honked at and a Marta bus, turning onto North Avenue, acted like it wanted to take off our rear end. It wasn't the usual Hump Evans driving.

"Some reason for this?" I was getting nervous.

"He gave me the route. He said he'd find us."

It was the third time around. I think we were wearing a groove in the road. Hump turned off North Avenue onto Parkway and headed for Ponce de Leon. Halfway down the block, on the right, a big black man stepped out of a doorway. The man looked about as big as Hump. He didn't move as well. The soft belly of good living had him. And he probably didn't work out the way Hump did.

He lifted a huge hand at us. Hump pulled to the curb. The man moved fast for his weight and the shape he was in. Across the weedy lawn, one step on the sidewalk, and he was in the back seat of the Buick.

"Drive around," he said.

"Any special place?" Hump had his eye on Cinch, watching him in the rear-view mirror.

"You pick it," Bill Cinch said.

That was the right answer. I moved my hand away from the towel. I could feel Hump relax.

Cinch was staring at me. I could see the bead sweat on his forehead.

"Jim Hardman," Hump said.

Wary eyes. "I see him."

We caught the red light at Ponce de Leon. Cinch leaned forward and placed his elbows on the seat back. I shifted toward the door to give him room. He was wider than most doors.

"I don't have much time," Cinch said.

"Do it any way you want to. Bill."

"It's got to be an agreement between us." He was talking to Hump but watching me.

Hump took a right when the light changed. "Set the terms."

"And he's covered too?"

The *he* was me. I let my eyes slide away from Cinch. It was Hump's move.

"He's covered by what I say." Maybe that wasn't strong enough. "He won't cross me."

"All right." Cinch lifted his elbows and leaned away. "This is the way I want it. My name's left out. I didn't give you this information. I don't even know you."

"Agreed." Hump looked at me.

I said, "Agreed."

"But when it's really over, if it's over and it works out, you can say I told you."

That was the kicker. He wanted it both ways. None of the blame if it didn't work out. Most of the credit if it did.

"It could get me killed and I know it."

I took one step back in my head and revised my thinking. He wanted the credit but he didn't want the beating or the bullet. Maybe he did know something worth our time.

"It stops here with me," Hump said.

"I'm going to trust you." Cinch dug in his shirt pocket and brought out a crushed pack of Camels. He lit one and I watched his hand. It had a tremble to it. "I was standing in the club doorway. That was right before the shooting. Two or three minutes, the way I figure it. This black LTD eases past the front of the club. It turns in the parking lot. It goes in, out of sight. A minute or so later, it eases back so the nose of the LTD is showing. I'm thinking about walking over and telling the driver he can't block the driveway. About that time the driver opens the door on his side. I think maybe the seat belt was caught in the door. Then the light's on and I get a look at him. I know that dude. I'm thinking about walking over and saying hello to him. About that time the shooting starts in the club. I never was good in math but I can add that high. I backed into the doorway and stayed there. Not much later I heard the car doors slam where the LTD was and it took off in the other direction."

"Who was it?"

"You see any of the others?" Hump said.

He answered Hump first. "I wasn't about to look. Soon as those shotguns went off, I knew seeing or being seen wasn't healthy."

"But you knew the driver."

"His name's Buck Thomas."

I said, "What's his real name?"

"That's his real name."

"No," I said, "apart from his nickname, what ... ?"

"His mama named him Buck. His daddy wasn't around to argue her out of it."

It was possible. I'd been to the Peach Bowl that year. The top pass catcher for Arizona was J. D. Hill. Sports writers wanted to know what J. D. stood for. It turned out it didn't stand for anything. That was his name. Just J. D. "Tell me what you know about him."

"Not much," Cinch said. "I worked a few times with him at one of the day-labor places. Drank with him a time or two after the jobs."

"Which day-labor shop?"

"A-1."

"He work in the rackets? Girls, numbers, drugs ... any of that?"

"Not that I know."

There went the possible tie-in. The two-day solution. I hadn't expected it anyway. "What else you know about him?"

"I think he was in the Marines. I heard he got a bad discharge."

"When was that?"

"Nineteen-seventy or 1971."

That put a federal handle on him. "Describe him."

"Might be six feet. Maybe one inch more. Might weigh a hundred and ninety."

"Dark or light?" I said.

"Dark, the real blood."

"Mustache?"

"Never knew him to wear one."

"Scars?"

"Not that you could see," Cinch said.

"Anything else you remember about him?"

"Wears this pinky ring. Gold. Supposed to have diamonds on it. They ain't real but they look real."

"That all?"

He nodded. I watched him in the rear-view mirror. He smoked the Camel down until it was about ready to burn his fingers. He rolled down the window and flipped the butt.

We'd passed the Plaza. Hump found a place to turn. He pulled into a driveway and waited until the traffic slowed and he could back out. He drove toward town.

"I'll drop you," Hump said. "You say where."

"It might be better you don't," Cinch said. "You got fifteen cents in change?"

I knew I did. I worked a handful of change from my pocket and picked out three nickels. I passed the bus fare to him and got his thanks. Then we were approaching the bus stop at North Highland and Ponce de Leon.

Cinch grabbed the door handle. "I'll get out here and catch the bus."

"It's no trouble to drop you," Hump said.

"It's better not to push our luck."

"We'll have that drink," Hump said.

"When the killing stops." Cinch waited until Hump was slowed, against the curb. He opened the door. Hump stopped. Cinch stepped out.

We'd caught the red light. I turned in my seat and looked back at Bill Cinch. He crossed the sidewalk and sat on the low brick wall there, head down. His crumpled pack of Camels was in one hand. He was shaking out a smoke when the light changed and we pulled away.

"That blows it wide open."

Hump's eyes were on the rear-view mirror. "You think we should have offered him some cash?"

"He got fifteen cents off me," I said. "I noticed you out-fumbled me on that."

Hump started to grunt at me and belched instead. That was that Pig's Place barbecue. It stayed with you for a week.

CHAPTER SEVEN

It was a long rest of the afternoon.

I couldn't reach The Man. I called his number four times. Each time a girl, on tape, said that the subscriber at this number was out for a few minutes. She didn't give any name at all. If, she said, at the sound of the tone I'd leave my name and phone number the subscriber would return my call.

I couldn't place her voice. I couldn't tell if she was black or white. If it mattered. Whoever she was she sounded like a graduate of the Royal Academy of Speech and Drama.

The first three calls, I played those straight. I left my name and phone number. The fourth time, after having to listen to Miss Proper Speech one more time, I said, "Goddamn it, Warden, this is important. Either call me or get screwed."

When he didn't return even that last call, Hump said he had better things to do with his time. He left for his apartment and I said I'd call him when and if I reached The Man.

Hump's attitude seemed the correct one. To hell with the crappy job. I called Marcy. I hadn't seen her for a couple of days. Usually if I didn't call, she'd call me. It was what I called her habit of checking my temperature. Or maybe this time there really was a new man in her office and she was gearing herself for some emotional blackmail. Some way of moving me into some nine-to-five job. One that I'd learn to like. So, I'd learn to do all those reflex words about how much I really liked my job. That kind of shit. Those lies.

Hump and I knew better than that. Which meant that we were smart in some ways that other people were dumb.

I told Marcy I was thinking about cleaning the spider webs out of the outdoor grill I had stored in the garage.

"Whatever for?" She was being coy. It made her happy.

"I hear that they have slaughtered a sick pig down the street and I thought I might grill the pig feet."

"The weatherman said it is going to rain."

I said, "Wait a minute" and looked out the bedroom window. It didn't look like rain at all. "Clear out there."

"It's on your head." She said she'd be over in an hour.

That gave me time. I made a run for The Superior on Highland. I'd stacked two packages of ribs in the cart before I remembered what I'd had for lunch. All that fuss and bother trying to reach The Man had made me forget. Still, I knew that spareribs were what Marcy would expecting. So, I left the ribs in and bought a jar of honey and a lemon. I added a bottle of Bengal Hot Chutney from the gourmet shelf and a bottle of a Pinot Chardonnay from the good wine shelf.

Home with time to spare. Still no sign of rain. I hosed out the grill and turned it upside down to drain. By then the big pot of water was at a rolling boil. I cut the spareribs into two- and three-rib sections and dropped them in the water. Twenty minutes at a boil and I cut the burner and let the ribs cool.

Back to the grill. I dried it with paper towels and laid a fire with last-year's charcoal. I doused the charcoal and got it burning. I was drinking a rum-and-tonic and putting the sauce together when I heard Marcy pull into the driveway.

I went on with the sauce. Marcy had her own key. Eight ounces of honey, the juice of one lemon and two tablespoons of hot curry powder. Stirring it, blending it between swallows of the rum and tonic.

"So much domesticity," Marcy said from the kitchen doorway.

"All for you," I said. I got my kiss and then I mixed her a rum-and-tonic. The first kiss tasted of cigarette smoke and toothpaste. After a rum-and-tonic she'd taste better.

Potatoes, washed and oiled and wrapped in heavy foil, hissed on the coals. Most of the grill was covered with ribs. It was getting dark and there was just enough light from the porch so that I could see to sauce the ribs and turn them now and then.

Most of the time I sat shoulder to shoulder with Marcy on the steps. Smelling her because the wind was blowing the charcoal smoke away, toward the terraced level. Smell of woman and a delicate perfume and of the lime oils around her mouth.

We were on our third rum-and-tonics when we saw the first fork of lightning in the distance. Another couple of minutes later and we got the first few drops of rain. Marcy grinned at me. "See?"

"Never happen."

I gave the ribs one more brushing with the sauce. I went into the kitchen and got the Pinot Chardonnay from the refrigerator and pulled the cork. A good scent to the cork.

A light rain was falling. I loaded my biggest platter with the ribs and placed the potatoes off to one side. Marcy stood on the porch and watched. "Wet ribs, Jim."

"The best kind."

We sat down to dinner. The light rain turned to a loud rattle and then a roar. The timing was perfect.

The Bengal Hot Chutney burned new tracks in my tongue. The honey-lemon-curry taste made me forget that it had turned into an all-pig day. We'd gone through about half the ribs and half the wine when I heard a knock at the door that wasn't either the rain or the wind that came with it.

I stopped by the bedroom for the .38. I held the gun down, flat against my leg. I stood away from the door. "Who is it?"

"The Man you've been calling," a man on the porch said. "And don't turn on the outside light."

I opened the door. A black I hadn't seen before stood there. He pushed in past me. He was short and broad-shouldered and wore a black hat pulled low over his eyes. The Man was a step behind him.

I closed the door after The Man was inside. My turn revealed the .38 in my hand. The black man made a reach for it. I shoved his arm away. "Goddamn it, get your hands off me." I looked at The Man. He was wearing a wet black raincoat. He dripped rain all over my living-room floor. "Tell him to back off."

"That's enough, Ray." The Man peeled off his raincoat.

I left him to decide where to put the coat. I went into the bedroom and put the .38 on the table next to the bed. When I returned, The Man was in the kitchen with Marcy. They were staring at each other like they couldn't decide how to start a conversation.

"This is Marcy," I said. "She's my lady."

The Man nodded. It was almost a bow. He could be courtly when he wanted to. It was all those damned period movies his mama must have taken him to when he was a boy. That and English drawing-room comedies.

"This is Warden Pike. I'm doing a job of work for him."

Marcy nodded. "It's nice to meet you, Mr. Pike."

"Please call me Warden," The Man said.

I put an arm around Marcy's shoulders and leaned over her. "I need to talk to Mr. Pike."

"I've just about finished."

I pulled back her chair. I refilled her glass with the wine. "Mind waiting in the bedroom for a few minutes?"

She said she didn't. I walked her into the bedroom and closed the door behind her. I returned to the kitchen and found The

Man seated at the table. He'd helped himself to a section of the ribs. "I hope you don't mind," he said. "I haven't eaten yet."

"Be my guest," I said. I got him a glass and poured him some of the wine. After I cleared Marcy's place, I passed him a fresh plate.

"A strange taste," he said.

I pushed the Bengal Chutney toward him. He poured it like catsup. "This goes well with it?"

"It's nothing without it," I said.

"You live well." He cleaned a rib bone and looked around. I passed him a wad of paper napkins. He wiped his fingers carefully before he picked up another rib cluster. "Very well indeed."

I could tell that he'd been impressed with Marcy. Most people were. He wasn't talking about the ribs or the wine. He was talking about Marcy.

His gun, Ray, leaned against the doorframe and stared at me. The way he watched me, you'd have thought I might attack The Man with a fork. "I need to talk to you," I said. "Without any other ears."

The Man shoved his chair away from the table. He edged past Ray and looked into the living room. He stepped out of my sight-line for a few seconds and I heard the TV sound come on. The Man returned. "Watch TV for a few minutes, Ray."

Ray moved away. The Man returned to his chair.

"That's better."

"You've been trying to reach me?"

"That's part of it," I said.

"I am not living there right now. You might say that … I am moving about the city."

"The Gibbs killing ran you?"

"He was one of my arms. It is only a matter of time before they try for me again."

"How am I supposed to reach you? The answering service sucks."

Using his fingers, he tore off a strip of pork and dipped it in the Bengal Chutney. "I will give you four numbers before I leave tonight."

"All right."

"You wanted to talk to me?" He checked his watch. "I am running on a fairly tight schedule."

"Hump and I stumbled across a name."

"What name?"

"The driver for the shotgun team last night."

"He's a dead man."

"No." I shook my head at him. "It's got to be my way. I need to talk to him. If I can't get the information I need in any other way, I might have to deal him his life."

"That's looking a bit far ahead."

"It's an option I want to keep." I lifted the wine bottle and split the last of it between my glass and his. "I don't want another P. J. Turner dead-ended."

"Very well, Mr. Hardman."

"His name is Buck Thomas."

"An in-town man?"

"I think so."

"Black like the other men in the team?"

I nodded.

"I will have it asked around."

"Soft talking," I said. "He'll drop in a hole if he hears you're asking."

"I will be very careful." He drained his wine glass. "A good wine."

I turned the wine bottle so that he could read the label. "Hump and I will try it our way. You try yours. One of us ought to get lucky."

"It won't be luck." He crossed to my sink and washed his hands. Drying them on a paper towel he said, "You'll have to tell me what the sauce was."

"Glad to."

I followed him into the living room. Ray jumped to his feet and switched off the TV set. He picked up The Man's raincoat and waited.

"You have a pen and paper?"

I went into the bedroom. When I opened the door, Marcy walked out and smiled at The Man.

"Have you finished your business?"

"I believe we have. Almost."

I returned with a pad and a pen. He took a card from his pocket and copied the numbers from the card onto my pad. When he passed the pad and pen to me, he said. "Of course, I wouldn't want these numbers to fall into other hands."

"No way," I said.

The Man turned to Marcy. That little suggestion of a bow. "They were excellent ribs, ma'am."

Marcy laughed. I watched The Man's back stiffen. He wasn't used to being laughed at.

"I did the ribs," I said.

"I see." That little bow again. "And I understand. A real lady shouldn't be bothered with such matters." He turned to Ray. Ray held open his raincoat and The Man twisted his way into it. Ray quick-walked to the front door and opened it. He turned and nodded at The Man. The Man pulled up his raincoat collar and followed him onto the porch. The rain was a steady, hard rattle.

I closed the door. The rain muffled.

Marcy smiled. "Where did you find him?"

"He found me."

"He's … he's …" Marcy fumbled for words. "He's unbelievable."

"How's that?"

"He's so quaint."

"Him?' I threw my head back and roared at the ceiling. Now she was the offended one. I choked off the laugh and explained. "You've heard Hump and me talking about The Man?"

"Yes."

"That's him. Warden Pike."

"My God." The breath went out of her.

When she'd recovered, we went back to the kitchen and finished our picnic. What was left of it.

Marcy stayed the night. The rain has a way of getting to her. The same way it gets to me. The rain womb.

CHAPTER EIGHT

The morning was gray and damp. The cool of May, the rain left from April.

I awoke early with Marcy and had coffee and an egg and toast with her. After she left, on her way to her apartment where she'd shower and change clothes before she left for her job with the Welfare Department, I folded the *Constitution* so I'd know where I'd stopped reading. I went back to bed. It was too damned early to be looking for anybody. People I'd be looking for would still be in bed anyway.

By noon, Hump and I were in the area around Pryor Street. For some reason a number of the day-labor offices are in that section of town, near the Fulton County Courthouse. I'd never figured out that reasoning. If there was any. But the yellow pages had listed the A-l Quick Labor Service with a Pryor Street address. That's why we were there.

We'd picked our time. By seven in the morning all the big jobs, the ones with the large crews, had been filled. The vans or the buses had departed for this part of town or that one. By noon, most of the offices would be empty except for the manager. He'd be drinking the last of the morning coffee. The bitter-dregs cup.

The gray had burned out of the sky. It was a beautiful Atlanta day. That was another plus. There wouldn't be any men sitting about the storefront shops and pretending to wait for a job that might come in late. That was the wintertime dodge. Then the labor pools were shelters, windbreaks and a place where you could cadge a cup of coffee if the manager knew you.

The hand-lettered sign in the A-1 window said they needed 107 men for work the next morning. It was always an uneven number. And it was usually a lie.

Hump waited outside. I went inside and tried out my Nationwide Insurance con. I had a stack of those new raised-lettering business cards in my jacket pocket. I whipped out one and leaned on the counter at the back of the long narrow room. While I waited for the manager or owner to notice me, I turned and had another look at the old black man I'd passed on the way in. He was seated at one of those refinished school desks. A paper cup of coffee balanced on the front edge of the desk while he bent over a section of the morning paper.

The manager or owner noticed me and got up from behind his desk. He was about my size but he had a beer belly that probably kept him from knowing when his shoes needed a shine. "I help you?" That was the polite that came from the jacket and the tie I wore. For all he knew, I could have been an investigator from the state Labor Department.

I turned the business card toward him and waited while he pressed his belly against the counter and stared down at it.

"Yeah?"

"Buck Thomas," I said.

"He's worked here some. Not lately."

"When was that?"

"The last time was back in February. I remember because he made trouble."

"How was that?" I turned on my elbow and looked at the old black man. His eyes were bad, I could see. He was holding the paper a couple of inches from his face. What I noticed was that he'd been moving the paper, making noise with it, and now he was still, body rigid.

"He walked off a job before it was done. That wasn't bad enough, so he talked two more guys into going with him. He said the job was dangerous."

"Was it?"

He stared at the business card once more. Insurance made him think hard for a few seconds before he answered. "Not really."

"You know how I can reach Buck?"

"You got a reason?"

I went into my con. Sometimes it was like pushing a button and hearing the tape run in me. This time it was that way. Smooth and easy. How Buck Thomas did some part-time work for a company that insured its workers with us. Driving a forklift. How he'd hurt his hand and quit. We needed to talk to him about the accident. Only thing was the address he'd given the company didn't check out. And, hell, there might even be some money in it for Buck. A few bucks. *A wink he understood.* Maybe not as much as the group policy called for. That was part of it. The rest was that my company needed to be sure that the warehouse had taken all the proper precautions. Otherwise they'd violated the terms of the insurance and they might have some problems.

He bought the story. The wink and the larceny helped. His business depended to some degree on a skim. "I'd like to help. It's just not the kind of business where we keep good records on addresses. And like I said, the last I saw of him and the last I want to see of him was back in February."

I put a finger on the business card and slid it back across the counter toward me. "That shoots today to hell." I thanked him and started away. Ahead of me, the old black was standing next to his desk. He was draining his coffee cup.

"The bar down the street. On the corner. Buck used to drink there. Might be somebody'd know him."

I nodded my thanks at the manager or owner. I reached the door. Going out, I heard the old black man say, "Mr. Taylor, I'm going out a few minutes. Any work comes in, I'll be back."

I didn't hear the answer he got. If he got one. I'd pulled the door closed behind me. I turned to my left and saw Hump with his back to the wall of the next-door building. He pushed away and flipped a smoke into the street.

"I can see ..." he said.

I touched his arm and we moved away from the storefront for a few feet. Then I stopped and turned back. The black man had followed me. Up close I could see that his brown work clothes were clean though they hadn't been pressed. His face was bony and the cheekbones high. I decided that there might be some Indian in him.

"Mister ...?"

I waited.

"You looking for Buck Thomas?"

"That's right."

"Might be I know something," he said.

"It too early in the day for a beer?"

"It's the right time." The old man had shifted. He was squinting at Hump.

"Only crackers ask that kind of question," Hump said.

Us against the cracker. That was the game Hump was playing. It was supposed to make the old man feel comfortable. But I'd been watching the old man's face and I thought what he needed was some alcohol in his bloodstream.

Fifty yards or so and we were in Shorty's Bar. It was desolation, the right time and the right place. Unwashed bodies and the smell of old sweat in clothing. I knew the area and the bar opened at seven in the morning. Men who didn't get work for the day and had the price had their beer breakfast at Shorty's. Now it was five hours later and most of the day's damage had been done.

I cleared a table of a pitcher, three glasses with foam dried in them, and the remains of a couple of bags of chips. Hump, seeing me start that, went to the bar and came back with three bottles of Bud. When Hump returned to the bar for his change the old man leaned toward me. "Might be this might be worth something to you. I ain't worked for two days."

"If it sounds good."

"How much?"

"A five," I said.

"Worth more than that." The old man lifted the bottle and drank from it, ignoring the glass. His bony adam's apple danced.

I got out a five and placed it on the table top. There was a saltshaker on the other side of the big ashtray. I reached for the shaker and planted it on top of the five and waited.

Hump slid into the booth next to me. The question started on his face: how's it going? He saw the five under the saltshaker and his face turned bland as oatmeal.

"Maybe you don't know anything," I said. "Maybe you're running a scam on me."

"Come on, Granddad," Hump said.

"I ain't your granddad," the old man said. It wasn't hard, it wasn't angry. It had some dignity in it. He put the Bud bottle to his mouth and had another long swallow. When he lowered the bottle he tipped his head at the five. "That and a pitcher?"

"All right," I said.

Hump seemed to be stuck with the leg work. He slipped out of the booth and moved to the bar. He said something to the bartender. He came back and pulled his Bud toward him. He poured about half of it back.

The bartender began filling a large pitcher. The old man saw that. He put the saltshaker aside and drew the five toward him. "I saw him last night."

I thought I'd been taken. "Where does he live?"

The old man folded the five and closed his hand over it. "That ain't what I know."

All right, by his rules. "Where'd you see him?"

"Where he hangs around mostly. It's a pool hall. He's there most every night, the way I hear it. Got his eye on a girl works there. He's been impressing her with a roll he's got on him."

"Where's this place?"

"Stewart Avenue."

"The address?"

"I don't know that," he said. "You know where that Salvation Army school is?"

I nodded.

"You know where Atlanta Tech is?"

I said I did.

"It's between them. On the right. Little place you got to watch for. Called The Spot. That's the name of it."

The bartender placed the pitcher on the bar and added three glasses. I decided it was my turn. I got out and paid for the pitcher and pushed two of the glasses back at him.

I put the pitcher in front of the old man. "He there in the daytime?"

"Him? He's a night man. You don't never see him in the day."

"What's the best time to find him there?" Hump finished his beer and pushed the bottle aside.

"Dark. Nine or ten."

I looked at Hump. He nodded. "I can find it."

I slid from the booth and stood looking down at the old man. "That five buys one more thing. You stay away from the pool hall tonight."

"Buck ain't nothing to me."

"Good."

"In fact, I don't even like him."

From outside, through the window, I watched him pour himself a glass from the pitcher. He was careful with the head. He didn't want to waste a bit of it.

Nine o'clock. Just getting dark. That was Daylight Savings Time for you. Dark when you got up in the morning and still light when you started thinking about bed.

I drove by Hump's apartment. He was waiting out front, seated on the steps, watching the cars go by and smoking a butt. It was a cloudy night. The air had a fine spray dampness to it. That didn't always mean that it was going to rain. Not in Atlanta.

I drove. Hump sprawled in the seat next to me. He was wearing dark slacks, a white knit shirt and a black windbreaker. "You in disguise?"

"I thought this was what the well-dressed pool hustler was wearing this year." He turned the collar of his windbreaker up. "You might call these my formal clothes."

"You shoot much?"

"I know how to hold the stick," Hump said. "That's it."

"Maybe you'd better watch then."

"Come in with me. You play."

I shook my head. I didn't know how rough the place was. It might get a lot rougher if I showed my white self in there. All that street anger and frustration, I didn't want it served up to me. I knew Hump wasn't serious in the offer. He knew as well as I did that that kind of crap just muddied the waters. Without it, it was simple.

"As planned?" Hump said.

We'd talked it out on the drive back from downtown, after we'd left the old black with his five and his pitcher of beer. Hump would hang around and locate Buck Thomas. He'd find him there or wait for him. He'd spend some time and then he'd join me across the street. That was the simple part of it. Beyond that it was foggy. Either we'd take him or we'd have to follow him.

It was a matter of a few words. Buck Thomas wouldn't want to say those words. Even a mumble in his sleep could get him dead. That was one leg of the nutcracker. The other leg was The Man. He didn't know about being on The Man's list. When he knew, if we offered him an open door, he might tell us what we wanted to know.

That simple.

We located The Spot and I drove past it a block or so. It was a narrow slot of a building. On one side was what had been at one time a drugstore. Now closed and boarded up. On the other flank was a dry-cleaning store. It was closed for the day, a night light burning in the rear of it.

Hump got out and walked toward The Spot. I went on another block and found a driveway and made my turn. It was full dark by the time I pulled to the curb across the street from the pool hall. Hump was already inside. I hadn't seen him on the street.

I settled down to the wait. No smoking. Scrunched down, head on the seat back, eyes just above the level of the car window so that I could watch the main entrance.

It was man traffic. I didn't see any women enter. Part of it was walking traffic. Ones and twos that appeared out of the darkness and were briefly in the light before they turned and vanished into the smoke and the noise.

I wanted a smoke. It was like a belly hunger. I couldn't risk it. There was too much regular in-and-out traffic. I fought it for a time and then I opened the glove compartment and dug about in there until I found part of a pack of gum. I chewed a couple of sticks and tried to relax.

It might be half the night. It might be thirty minutes.

That was the bad part. Not knowing.

It was after eleven. I was stomping my feet to wake them up when I saw Hump come out of the pool hall. He carried a small paper bag in one hand. At the opposite curb, he stopped and looked in both directions before he crossed to my Ford. I was ready for him. I unlocked the door on the driver's side and slid into the passenger seat. I ducked my head when he opened the door and stepped in, that brief moment when the inside of the car was lighted, and then he was behind the wheel and the light was out.

"You been watching?"

"Napped some," I said.

"You see a dude in a red-and-green plaid jacket? Entered about half an hour ago?"

"No."

"He's our man. Remember what the old man said about Thomas being interested in a girl works there? I got to talking to her. The dude in the plaid jacket comes in and she leaves me like a shot. And I heard her call him Buck."

"The rest match what Bill Cinch told us?"

"On the nose." The paper bag rustled in his lap. He tore it away and held up two cans of Bud. "Thirsty?"

"Thoughtful of you."

He passed a can to me. I popped the top and felt the foam pour over the edge and onto the front of my pants. That was all right. The dry-cleaning bill would be balanced by the taste, the coolness. I'd been thirsty.

"We wait?"

"Unless you've got a better idea," I said.

He didn't.

The next hour the crowd in the pool hall started to thin. Ones and twos. The way they'd come. There was some yelling on the street and we watched a mock scuffle between a couple of young studs. Nothing to it. They pulled their punches. It was a ballet for drunks. It ended as abruptly as it began. Some back-slapping and they walked off in opposite directions, yelling at each other. *Sheeeet* and *motherfucker.*

Exactly at one a.m. the "Pabst on Draft" sign stopped flickering and went dark. Hump's breathing was a shade too regular. I gave him a poke in the ribs.

"Huh?"

"Coming out soon."

"I'm watching. You think I'm sleeping?"

A black man in a fancy jacket walked from the pool hall. He turned and held out a hand to a woman with bowed legs. She looked in her mid-twenties.

"That him?"

"That's the jacket. It's dim out there."

A beefy man in a bartender's apron followed them to the walk. They talked for a minute or so and then the bartender backed inside and closed the front door to the pool hall. The man in the fancy jacket put an arm around the waist of the girl and they headed down the street to our left. They passed the closed drugstore and stepped off the curb. In the near part of the next block there were two or three cars parked. I watched through the rear window as the man released the girl and moved around and got behind the wheel of what looked like a Skylark.

Traffic was slow on Stewart. Hump leaned forward and reached for the ignition key. I said, "Give it a second more."

It was just as well. The Skylark fired up and Thomas did a U-turn that almost clipped a low-branched dogwood on our side of the street. Hump ducked and gave me a shove as the headlights ran up the tail of my Ford.

I gave him half a block and said, "Go."

We pulled into the street and loafed along about a block behind. A few blocks and a battered pickup truck sandwiched itself between us and I tapped Hump and he pulled in closer.

The pickup stuck there until we reached Five Points. It took a right on Decatur. That left us in the open. Hump eased down and let a white high-wheeled pimpmobile with what looked like fur seat covers loop us and ride the Skylark's tail.

It was a straight shot through downtown Atlanta. Maybe Buck Thomas was sightseeing. The pimpmobile took a lift and headed for an all-night diner on North. The Skylark continued on. A curving right onto Ponce de Leon.

I touched Hump on the shoulder. "Let it spread out."

It was a risk. Always a chance we'd miss a green and hit a red. When we hit Ponce de Leon the Skylark was edging into the center turn lane. The light was green but changing. Hump saw that and took a sharp right into the bank parking lot. That led to the driveway and the series of drive-in windows. Hump pulled through one of the drive-in slots and hit Piedmont. He took another turn, a left, and we could see the taillights of the Skylark about a block away. We had a green and we crossed Ponce de Leon and made up some of the gap. A few more blocks and Thomas pumped the brakes and hit his turn signal. Hump slowed and as we went by. I saw that it was one of the old apartment houses. The Skylark was parking.

I pointed to the curb about half a block away. "Park it, Hump." He did. He cut the engine and the lights. Piedmont was one-way. We sat there for ten minutes. Another five minutes. The Skylark didn't come out of the drive.

"Around the block," I said.

We circled the block and went toward the apartment-house driveway. One of my fears, the reason we'd spent those ten minutes parked down the street, was that Buck Thomas might be just dropping the girl off at her apartment.

Hump turned into the driveway. The Skylark was still there. Hump stopped with his headlights on the tag numbers. I got out a pen and wrote them down on a scrap of paper bag.

"We go in after him?"

"Not in the dark," I said.

Hump made a turn and headed back toward Piedmont. "What do we do?"

"Leave it for the night." I didn't want to tell him that I hadn't decided.

"The way the girl acted he's parked for the night."

It wasn't going to be an easy decision. Whether we came back in the morning and waited for Thomas and followed him about until he got vulnerable and gave us a chance at him. Or whether we placed the phone call to The Man and left it to him. However he wanted to do it.

One thing I knew. I wasn't going to blunder about any dark apartment house trying to find a man so we could ask our questions. Not when that man might be armed.

It wasn't good sense.

And in this dark-world business, if you can call it that, the ones who stayed alive had good sense. Or were lucky. Or both.

CHAPTER NINE

The list of phone numbers The Man had given me had time brackets. The first one was marked for six a.m. to noon, the next one for noon to six p.m., the third for six p.m. to midnight and the final one for the hours from midnight to six a.m.

I sat at the kitchen table and stared at the list. It didn't make much sense to me. Hump pushed a beer toward me and mixed himself a J&B-and-rocks.

"I'm beered out." He sat down and stared at me. "You decide anything yet?"

"There's some cold blood in Warden Pike."

"I get a vote?"

I nodded. I lifted the bottle of Bud and sucked at it.

"I say we spend the day trying to get close to Buck Thomas. We give it a good shot." He sipped his scotch. "It doesn't turn out and we pass it over to Pike. But not until then."

It was the risky way. It was, I guess, the same way I felt. I picked up my Bud and the list and pushed back my chair.

"How do you vote, Jim?"

"With you." I waved the list of telephone numbers at him. "I'm going to check these out."

I sat on the edge of the bed and dialed the first three numbers. After each dialing, I let the phone ring a dozen or so times before I decided that there wasn't going to be an answer. Then I got the operator on the line and read her the first number.

"I'm having trouble reaching the party," I said. I smiled to myself. I was beginning to talk like a telephone operator.

"I'll try it for you, sir." They're very polite in Georgia.

It rang about ten times before she gave up.

"He's supposed to be there," I said.

"That number is a pay phone," the operator said.

I thanked her and broke the connection. Stranger and stranger. What the hell was Warden Pike doing? I dialed the number in the midnight-to-six-a.m. slot. It rang three times.

"Yeah?"

"I want to speak to Pike."

"Who?"

"The Man," I said.

"Name and number," the man on the other end said.

I gave them to him and hung up. I carried my beer back into the kitchen. I had a look in the refrigerator. I didn't find anything worth the trouble. A piece of Black Diamond cheese turning green. A half-pound of good salami just getting slick. Last week's tuna-fish salad that floated in moisture.

"What'd you find?"

I gave it up and closed the refrigerator door. "I think the Man's moving around. I don't know how." I gestured with the list. "I think these are pay phones. All of them. He parks somebody at an out-of-the-way pay phone for six hours. All calls come through are passed on to him."

"It's absurd enough to make sense to Pike."

I looked at the kitchen clock. Two-forty-three. "Speaking of him, I put in a call."

"You called Pike?"

"I know how we're doing. I thought I'd see how it was going for him."

"Scared me there for a minute." Hump passed me and tipped some scotch in his glass and added two or three ice cubes from the refrigerator before he returned to his chair. "I thought maybe you didn't believe in the democratic process."

"Me?" I grinned at him.

The phone rang five minutes later.

"Yes, Mr. Hardman."

"Just checking in," I said.

"This time of night?"

"I was having trouble sleeping." I moved the phone away from my mouth and burped. "Everything all right at your end?"

"There is some discomfort," The Man said. "It was to be expected, I suppose."

"No place like home," I said.

"The wheelman …"

"Buck Thomas."

"How is the investigation going?"

"It's a good lead, I think."

"But you haven't found him?"

"Not yet," I said.

"You're lying, Mr. Hardman."

"What?"

"You're lying."

I heard a click and the line went dead. I said, "Shit" and started dialing the midnight-to-six-a.m. number. Halfway through I stopped and replaced the receiver.

I sat there for a time before I went into the kitchen and told Hump that I thought we were out of work again.

Hump yawned down at his scotch. "Screw the job."

It was 3:30 before Hump lost his taste for J&B. Instead of the drive back into town he settled for my sofa.

Marcy woke me at 8:15. If I'd been able to find my watch, I'd have known it was her. At 8:15 she was five or ten minutes away from her everyday drive downtown to work.

"I tried to reach you all night, Jim."

"We were on a job." I rubbed my eyes and felt the grit roll off my knuckles.

"Until one a.m.?"

"Later than that."

"Is it the same job? The one for that nice Mr. Pike?"

"For Pike," I said. I didn't feel up to a discussion of Pike's virtues or lack of them.

"How long is that job going to last?"

"It's over." I found my watch. Yes, it was a bit after 8:15. The woman on the phone had to be Marcy. It couldn't be a wrong number. Or a mash call.

"Then you can take me to dinner tonight." It should have been a question but it wasn't.

"Any special place?"

"The Abbey."

That nudged me. I was almost fully awake. At least I was awake enough to do the figures in my head. Any way you added it up it was thirty dollars a person and that meant two for sixty dollars. Without the tip that had to be large enough to be divided between the three or four waiters, wine stewards and such that took turns swooping and pouncing on you. "All right, Marcy. What time?"

"Eight should be fine. You'll call for the reservation?"

I said I would. "I'll see you here at seven-thirty?"

"No," she said. "You can pick me up here." *Here* was her apartment. A faceless acre or two of small apartments. Trees planted so recently that you couldn't expect shade for another ten years. Only in the last year or so had the grass covered the scraped ground enough so that the water in the swimming pool wasn't red-clay-dust red.

"Aw … Marcy."

"Seven-thirty?"

I said I'd be there.

It was, I guess, time for it. It happened every six or eight months. Something happened and it started her thinking. *I wasn't taking her seriously enough. I was taking advantage of her. I wasn't treating her like the lady she really was. It was time to remind me what our relationship should be and had been.*

In a few days it would pass. It always had.

I settled back into bed. The door to the living room was cracked a few inches. I could hear the bull elephant snore, the window rattling, from Hump.

Past the slitted blinds, I could see the cool May morning with a stir of wind in the green trees.

Getting fired isn't my idea of a way to end a night or begin a day.

It colored it blue. Dark. No matter that we hadn't wanted it, that we'd been pushed into it.

Hump and I were glum over a late breakfast at the Majestic. The morning paper didn't interest either of us. And when I dropped him in front of his apartment house, he gave me a see-you-sometime wave and started up the steps.

I headed home. I didn't get there. I got about halfway and then I changed my mind. I made a turn across a service-station apron and headed back.

It seemed different in the daytime. It was the change that light gives to a street. The shadows are gone, all the dark voids. When I swung left into the driveway, at first, I thought I'd picked the wrong one. Then I saw the Skylark parked where Buck Thomas had left it the night before. The same place. I passed it and found a slot two cars over. I pulled in and cut the engine. I sat there and tapped the steering wheel. There wasn't any reason to move either way. I'd come this far without knowing why I'd come at all.

Maybe in the beginning I'd thought about going against The Man. I'd find the right apartment and I'd pass the word. It was dangerous. Get out of town.

In the hard world that made a pussy out of me. No eye for an eye. Smiley Gibbs was dead. That meant Buck Thomas owed an eye. No way around that.

Or I could act like I was still working. I could think up some scam and get close to Buck Thomas. I could start the wheels going and I could call Hump. *Yes, Mr. Pike, what you want to know is…*

That was two. The third option made more sense than the others. I could back out and drive home and forget it.

Five minutes passed. Another five. And then the decision was made for me. It began, in the distance, as a low wail. It could have been heading in any direction. I think I knew better. When it was closer, I knew that it was an ambulance. Still, even as the ambulance turned from Piedmont, it wasn't a pure siren sound. It was a mixture.

I got out of my car and stood and watched the ambulance jerk to a stop in the driveway. The siren guttered and choked to an end and I picked out the rest of it. There was a police siren still screaming a block or two away.

The attendants were out of the ambulance in a fresh early-morning trot. While they opened the rear doors and lifted out a rolling stretcher, I edged toward the front entrance to the apartment house. I had the door open when they reached it and the lead attendant nodded his thanks at me. I let them through and with one look down the drive I followed them. The police cruiser pulled in behind the ambulance. The siren wheezed and I was left with the echo of both of them. Rattling around between my ears.

The attendants were halfway up the first flight of stairs when I started after them. I took the steps three at a time and got on the heels of the back man. He turned and looked at me. Maybe he thought I was the manager. He didn't seem concerned. He didn't tell me to go away.

When we reached the third floor, they lowered the rolling stretcher and the lead man pulled it with a strap. Far down the hall, a dumpy white woman in a pink robe was positioned in an open doorway.

"Here," she shouted. "I called you."

I followed the stretcher. I stopped in the doorway next to the dumpy lady. I looked into the apartment. A black woman in a short half-slip and a bra slumped in a stuffed chair. The right side of her jaw was swollen. Broken, I guessed.

The ambulance attendants positioned the stretcher and took the woman by the arms and helped her out of the chair. When she stood I could see the bowed legs. The face hadn't told me anything. The legs did. She was the woman who'd left the pool hall with Buck Thomas.

I turned to the dumpy woman. "What happened?"

"Early this morning I heard this noise. I thought she and her boyfriend were having a fight."

The attendants helped her onto the stretcher and spread a sheet over her. She was moaning, a low almost musical hum.

"I didn't think anything about it," the dumpy woman said. "It happened before, you know."

I nodded.

"A few minutes ago, I came out to look for my paper and she was standing in the doorway. Hurt like that."

"She say anything?"

"All she said was that somebody had broke in."

I looked into the apartment again. The attendants passed us, pulling the stretcher. A uniformed policeman appeared at the head of the stairs. He stood there and waited until the attendants reached him.

"What happened to the boyfriend?"

"I asked her that. All she'd say was that they took him."

The policeman went down the stairs with the attendants and the stretcher. I walked over and looked at the apartment door. It hadn't been forced. But it was the kind of lock you could trip with a credit card.

I nodded my thanks to the lady and walked down to the first floor. I stood in the doorway until both the ambulance and the police cruiser left.

It wasn't long.

And then I drove home and called the Abbey and made a reservation for two.

CHAPTER TEN

It was a mark of how important I was that the maitre'd led us through all the choice seats and up a flight of stairs to a balcony that overlooks the central dining area at the Abbey. Maybe by itself that wasn't all bad. From that position, we could look down and see what everybody had on their plates. But there was one more consideration. We were right next to the lady harpist who furnished all the dinner music. The back of Marcy's chair was only inches away from the front edge of the harp. That close, we had to listen to the concert whether we wanted to or not. And the only time we had for conversation was when the lady harpist took a break.

The Abbey used to be a church, Unitarian I think, and when the church decided to move from that part of town into the suburbs, they sold the land and the church building. The people who bought it did a minimum of decoration and they put the waiters in monk's cassocks. Satisfied that that was grand they jacked the prices up to the roof level and opened the doors for business.

I let Marcy select the dinner. Crabmeat in an avocado half. Small slices of pork flamed in vodka, fresh asparagus and fresh mushrooms sautéed in butter and white wine.

I had to smell the cork of an ordinary bottle of white burgundy. I know all the reasons for it but I always feel a little like I'm posing for an ad. But I did it and I nodded and I had a sip of the cork glass and Marcy seemed pleased with me. We were getting along well. I guess it wasn't supposed to last. The harpist returned from her break and Marcy, who'd moved her chair back, now had to move it in toward the table. It was that close. The harpist appreciated it and she asked Marcy if there was any music in particular that she wanted to hear. Marcy passed it on to me and I asked if the harpist knew "Turkey in the Straw."

The harpist leaned away from our table, laughing. It was a joke, right? A big joke? And Marcy, instead of being amused, stared at me like she'd just caught me exposing myself to little children on the schoolyard.

The bill came to a bit over fifty-five dollars. I added another ten for the platoon of waiters and wine stewards and dessert chefs. On the way down the stairs I turned and saluted the lady harpist. She nodded and gave me a plastic flower smile, all without missing a string.

Goodbye, goodbye, redneck. *Plunk.*

At Marcy's door, it was all very proper. Thank you and she'd had a nice evening. The dinner was fine. All that and she didn't even ask if I wanted to come in for a drink or a cup of coffee.

It was part of those six-or eight-month blues that I had to go through along with those high-school dates.

I guess I was deep in that, the feeling that I'd spoiled it for her by being a smartass with the harpist. Not that it mattered. I really knew that I wasn't supposed to do anything right. That was our "set," our position, until Marcy lived past those blues. They were the I'm-gettin-older-and-I-don't-like-my-life-and-you're-not-helping-much blues. So, I was deep in that and I was trying to estimate how long it would be before she recovered and we could go back to being friends and lovers.

I'd parked in the drive and I was cutting across the lawn when the two men stepped out of the shadows at the driveway corner of the house. I just saw the big shapes and I turned and set myself and said, "Oh, shit" out loud. It just wasn't one of my better days but if I was lucky, I could give one of them a limp or a bruise or two.

I brought up my hands and closed them into fists.

"Come on, Hardman," one of the men said, "we're not going to mug you."

I recognized the voices and dropped my hands. The lead man was Baylor, the cop from Intelligence with the smoker's hoarseness. The other shadow shape, I saw, belonged to his partner, Franklin.

"We've been waiting for an hour," Franklin said.

"It must be important then."

"Something we want you to look at," Baylor said.

They flanked me and we walked across the lawn and down into the street. They'd parked their car one door down from my house.

"Buck Thomas," I said.

The black man was slumped, head pressed down on his chest. He was seated in one of those cheap outdoor folding chairs. His hands were taped to the arm rests. He was dressed only in boxer shorts and a V-neck T-shirt. The shirt wasn't white anymore. It was splattered with blood.

"I think you know who he is," Baylor said behind me. His voice almost echoed in the hollow empty building.

"Buck Thomas," I said.

"Why?"

"He was the wheelman for the Smiley Gibbs killing."

The drive had been through desolate slum country. The rotted heart of the city. The blighted part of it. Franklin had parked in the recessed entrance to a warehouse, next to the loading ramp. There were FOR LEASE signs all over the building.

Baylor opened a door and we were inside. There was a strong smell of dust and rodent shit and something else that turned out to be Buck Thomas.

Behind us, Franklin had found the light switch. On both sides, there were a series of wired-in storage bins. At the rear of the huge room was a sliding door that opened wide enough to let a moving van in.

Buck Thomas was in the third storage bin to the right.

I stepped away. I'd seen enough. "Why'd you come for me?"

"You match the description of somebody who was playing detective to some lady early this afternoon on Piedmont."

"That's true."

I walked out of the bin. I wanted that behind me. I went as far as the sliding door. The concrete floor was dusty. I could see shoe prints in the dust and, starting at the sliding door, the tracks of some tires. There was also a smear of oil. I touched the toe of my shoe to the oil. It was still damp, still slick.

I walked back to Baylor and Franklin. They were waiting at the entrance to that storage bin. Baylor turned and dipped his head toward Buck Thomas. "Pike do that?"

"I don't know." I waited. "I didn't finger him for Pike."

"Ask him for us," Baylor said.

I shook my head. "I think I'm fired, as of last night."

"Why?"

"I'd located Thomas and I said I hadn't."

"He knew better?"

"Or he guessed," I said.

"Why'd you lie?"

"That." I nodded at the storage bin where the body was. "I was afraid of that."

Baylor turned and slapped the wired bin with the palm of his hand. The wire rang. It continued to vibrate. More dust swirled in the tight-in air. I sniffed and felt it beginning to cake in my nose. It reminded me of summer in New York.

Baylor's head was down. He was staring at the dust wire marks on his hand. "You should have called me when you located him. He might be alive and he might be talking."

I didn't argue it. There were arguments I could have made. That Buck Thomas would have been a quick phone call away from release if he'd been picked up. That the eyewitness had a bad case of the shys. All that. Instead I shrugged and said, "It was becoming a one-way street."

"Huh?"

"You never called back."

"That the bonus you promised me?"

We were headed back to my house. There hadn't been much to say the first part of the drive. Whatever they were thinking they weren't sharing with me. And, I guess, I didn't want to say what I was thinking either.

One of the two things had happened, I was fairly certain. Either The Man had us tailed and I'd been a goat and led them straight to Buck Thomas or they'd found him in their own way. What one man can do another one can do just as well. Something like that. No, I don't think we'd been tailed. I threw that out. It had to be the other way. They'd found him through their own sources after I'd given them a name. Maybe they'd been sitting in their car in that dark parking lot outside the apartment house on Piedmont. The long evening's wait for Buck Thomas to arrive. And when he'd arrived, Hump and I had been there minutes later. A flash of our headlights over his tag numbers and somebody'd said, "That's interesting," and either they'd known my old Ford or they'd taken down my tag numbers and passed them back to The Man. With his "in" it was short-time work to find out who'd been tailing Buck Thomas.

And The Man had known I was lying when I called.

"What bonus?"

I was riding in the back seat. Franklin was driving. Baylor put a thick arm on the seat back and looked over it.

"You know. The bonus you promised you'd pay me with when I told you about the Smiley Gibbs killing."

"That one?" Baylor laughed. Franklin joined in and thickened the sauce. That ran down to a cough and cleared his throat. "There was something. I don't think you'd be interested now. The bloodbath's about to start. You're well out of it."

"Tell me anyway. It'll give me something to think about while I spend the rest of the summer watching the Braves."

"Tell him," Franklin said.

"We got a taste. A hint. We think it's California. The new-style dudes."

"What is?" I didn't feel very bright. I felt sluggish. I didn't bother to check my watch. It wasn't that late.

"The takeover try. Vice picked up this Hollywood surfer type and passed him over to us. Suntanned and sun-bleached hair. Muscles on his muscles and a taste for little boys."

"Why Vice?" It wasn't their province. It wasn't usual.

"They just stumbled on him. They knew I was interested."

"Come on," Franklin said. "You know everybody has got a right to do their thing. It's a part of the Bill of Rights."

"And everybody has got a right to have a pocketful of candy and an open fly and park across the street from the school."

I knew I'd have to wait. They were playing games. They'd been partners so long they passed time by doing word games. One would take one side and the other would come down hard on it.

"Having a pocketful of candy and an open fly don't mean he's gay," Franklin said.

"Anyway," Baylor said to me, "this Muscle Beach type gets scared and starts sweating."

"With reason," Franklin said.

"He's from the West Coast. Long Beach originally but now out of L.A. He tells us he got recruited to move to Atlanta. He'd been managing some girl show and a couple of bathhouses out there. Those anything-you-can-pay-for places."

"You don't like anybody," Franklin said. "First you don't like guys who like little boys and now you got something against the girls too."

"The more he talks the more it looks like he's opening a can of fat worms for us. Now it begins to look like fishing time. It seems somebody on the West Coast took a long look at Atlanta and decided it was ripe. A police department with problems, a city trying to be a tourist and convention city as a way of trying to save itself. That rotten stew. So, they moved in. They open a bathhouse or two. They hire the best lawyers and fight the city to a standstill. It's a win because the city can't close them down. Then they do the next step. They open a bare-ass show. Police close it the first day. Turns out they don't serve booze or beer. Just soft drinks and a buffet. That's for the admission price. Since there's no liquor license involved there's no way the city can touch them."

"High flying," Franklin said.

"But you know the types. They get one chunk of the action and they want it all. Before they moved in, they knew the territory. They had a good research job. Since Atlanta's an open city, they didn't have to ask their way in. They ran off some of the Dixie Mafia types and they bought the others. The first plan was to stay away from The Man's operation. Just let it be. But they kept looking at the drugs, the gambling, the numbers, and they decided they'd got the first piece of cake easy. They fooled themselves into believing the rest would be, too."

They reached my house. Franklin pulled into the driveway behind my Ford.

"The first move was bringing in Turner from Detroit."

I found a Pall Mall in my shirt pocket. I lit it and blew the smoke through a partly opened back window. "No California hitters?"

"Oh, they've got them all right. This was sleight of hand, what you might call misdirection. If it worked, fine. Nobody cared then. If it didn't work, all the signs would point in the wrong direction. Toward the Midwest. Also, aside from that, Turner had a good batting average."

"And the hit on Smiley Gibbs?"

"Misdirection too. A team of blacks. What did The Man think first? That some of his own boys might be after him?"

"He considered it," I said. I left out the fact that I'd suggested it to him as a possibility.

"Then that part worked."

"Confusion to their enemies," I said. "What next?"

"What you saw back there. Lots more of it. Street cleaning. We sweep up the bodies."

"No way to stop it?"

"You mean like giving everybody six hours to get out of town?"

"Who's running the California thing?"

"Here in Atlanta? A man named Matt Turlow."

"Mob?"

"Mafia? No. It's Wasp. No blood oaths. None of that. Just good green money."

I hit the door handle. "Good thing I'm out of it."

"You hope," Franklin said.

I stopped with the door open a couple of inches. The overhead light made all three of us blink. "What does that mean?"

"You better run an ad in the paper and say you don't work for Pike anymore. It might take a day or two for it to go through the grapevine."

"That's true." I felt the skin sting and started to sweat.

"I'll see it gets passed," Baylor said. "It'll be full payment from me."

"Thanks." I stepped out and started to close the door. Instead, I leaned back into the interior of the car. "The guy did the talking, the one who liked little boys, what happened to him?"

"That was sad," Franklin said. "He's in the hospital. He tripped getting out of a police car and broke his collarbone and both knee caps."

"All that?" I waited.

Baylor had turned face forward. All I could see of him was the back of his head. It was Franklin who was twisted in his seat, looking back at me. His face was bland, smoothed over.

"It turned out the school where he'd been hanging around just happened to be the same one where Baylor's seven-year-old-boy goes."

"Small world," I said.

"Ain't it?"

I closed the door. Franklin backed out of the drive. I went into my house and mixed myself a J&B-and-rocks. I sat down in front of the TV and watched Dorothy Lamour and Jon Hall running around between plastic jungle flowers. I never did understand what the plot was. A second drink and it didn't matter that much.

A volcano was scaring the hell out of the natives when I cut the set off and made myself a third drink and carried it into the bedroom. I undressed and sat on the edge of my bed. I took the phone off the hook and listened to the hum.

By the time I cut off the lights and fell back into the bed, I was used to the hum.

CHAPTER ELEVEN

The Houston Astros were in town for a three-game series. I called Marcy at the office and found that she was still in the same funk. She said something about having a headache and something about having to do two weeks of laundry. If I'd given her more time, I think she'd have discovered a backache or a toenail that hurt as well.

So I called Hump. He was coming out of a late-afternoon daze. It was the result of drinking his lunch at some downtown bar that specialized in young spring lamb girls. He'd had a great time but then the girls had gone back to work and he'd gone home for his afternoon nap.

Hump said, "Why the hell not?" and I drove over and parked in the lot next to his apartment house and we rode to Atlanta Stadium in his Buick.

It was a good game. The Braves, under new ownership, had traded away some ballplayers who could hit but had bad attitudes for some other ballplayers who couldn't hit but had good attitudes and probably loved their mothers and God knows what else.

Niekro pitched. His flutterball takes so long to reach the plate that you feel you have time to drink half a beer and smoke half a cigarette before it gets there.

The Braves tried to give the game to the Astros in the ninth but the Astros didn't want it, either and the Braves won and I flattened out the last of my beer cups under my heel and watched the crowd make their stampede for the exit ramps. It was a good crowd for Atlanta, somewhere on the other side of 14,000.

Hump had recovered from his nap. He'd poured back about half a gallon of that high-priced beer and his hand didn't shake anymore and his eyes were bright. I could see that he was thinking of the night ahead now that he felt better.

I'd spoiled it some with my account of the early-morning guided tour of the warehouse and the talk I'd had on the way back with Baylor and Franklin. I'd done that during the slow moments that a baseball game seems constructed of.

"You didn't tell me about your buddies," Hump had said.

"The two from Intelligence? I meant to. And the deal made, it seemed a fair trade at the time."

And then we'd got involved in the ninth-inning try to give the game to the Astros and it wasn't until the aisles were clearing that Hump asked his real question. "You hear much from Pike?"

"I don't expect to. Unless he wants some of his money back."

"He can have it," Hump said. "At least what's left of it."

I felt the same way. Screw the money. What bothered me and what bothered him was that we'd been involved, by giving him a name, by running the hunt for Buck Thomas, in The Man's warehouse butchery. It didn't swallow well. It sat on my stomach like an ice cube I'd gulped down by mistake.

"Matt Turlow, huh?"

"That's the name. You know of him?"

We followed the stragglers up the aisle and down the curving ramps that led to the ground-level gates. There wasn't any reason to hurry. Even 14,000 at an Atlanta game made a traffic jam on all the streets heading downtown.

"I thought I'd get the name right," Hump said.

We passed through the gate and crossed the stadium parking lot and dodged traffic to the off-the-premise lot where we'd paid some black kid a dollar to make sure we still had tires and hubcaps when we got back from the game. We got into the car. The black kid had disappeared.

It was still early. The game had started at 7:35 and it was only 10:29 by my watch.

"That bare-ass show. You know which one it is?"

"Not that I've ever been there," Hump said.

"Of course not."

"It's probably a place called The Bird's Nest."

"Was a time I used to go to a titty show now and then." I lit a smoke and passed the package to Hump.

"Before Marcy?"

I nodded. After Marcy had returned to town, and we'd taken up again, it had somehow seemed unfaithful of me to go about looking at strange bodies. No matter how new or how beautiful the bodies were.

"Hardman, if you are thinking what I think you are thinking, I'd better do you my five-minute lecture that talks you out of it."

"Me? I'm just bored."

"How was dinner last night?"

"It was the most expensive high-school date I've had in twenty-five years."

"That shit, huh?"

"One more time," I said.

Hump leaned over and turned the ignition key. We pulled out of the empty lot. Hump risked a fender bulling his way into the stadium traffic. After that it was a straight shot downtown. Bumper to bumper.

The Bird's Nest had been, perhaps a year ago, a stripper bar called Andy's Weather Vane. I'd been in the place a time or two then. I'd take a casual look at the skin, have a drink and move on. It wasn't, even then, my idea of a neighborhood tavern.

Andy's had been famous for a red-haired stripper named Dora. She'd had breasts like two of those round loaves of sourdough bread. But she'd moved on and there'd been some story of a fight in Dora's dressing room. The drummer in the three-piece band had found Dora mouth-to-muff with his wife. The fight had been between the drummer and his wife.

The layout of the club hadn't changed that much. The table placement was about the same from what I remembered. The bar was over against the right side wall and the only difference was that they'd taken the stools away. If you wanted to watch the show from the bar, you had to stand or lean.

The curved end of the bar, the one closest to the main entrance, was now the buffet. It was covered with a paper tablecloth and there were a few platters of cold cuts arranged on it. After I'd popped for the entrance price, $7.50 each, I'd drifted past the display. There were a few slices of salami, some sliced ham with a green sheen to it, some slices of American cheese still in the plastic wrappers, some limp lettuce leaves and a few tomato slices floating in their own warm juice. In the center of those platters there was about a five-pound tub of Mrs. Kinser's brand potato salad.

The bread was a loaf of Colonial white. No rye. No choice.

I passed up the buffet and leaned an elbow on the bar. The bar might have been the right height for seated people. For standing or leaning it wasn't that comfortable. Maybe that was the idea.

The shill girl outside, not knowing we were going in anyway, had said the show was about to start. It didn't look that way from where I stood. The stage was dark. Light from the wall fixtures spilled far enough so I could see the red, white and blue bunting at the front edge. In the dead center of the bunting there was an American eagle, made out of cardboard, that looked like it had a broken wing.

The bartender had been at the other end of the bar stocking the drink box. He edged our way. He wore white trousers and a pale blue shirt that was unbuttoned down to the navel. Some kind of silver medal dangled there, against a dark suntanned and almost hairless chest. "Anything you gentlemen want," he said, "as long as it's a soft drink."

"Coke," I said.

Hump walked over from his look at the buffet and nodded.

The bartender reached into the drink box and brought up two cans of Coke. He popped the tabs and pushed the can toward us. No glasses.

Hump had a sip of the Coke. "When does the show start?"

The bartender looked at his watch. He said, "Soon." He moved away like he thought we might insist upon knowing how soon.

I leaned on the bar and did a head count. A party of four at the front table, the one closest to the stage. Tourists, I thought, from the leisure suits and the loud shirts. And one of them was even eating a sandwich. If it was the ham, he might regret it early in the morning.

A black man sat at one of the side tables. He was still dressed in tan work clothes and heavy shoes. A few minutes later, when he came to the bar for another soft drink, I read his shoulder patch and saw that he worked for the city sewer department.

There were three young kids at a table in the center of the room, behind the one where the tourists were. They looked about eighteen or nineteen and they might be college students or they might be high school. Maybe they'd driven in from some suburb like Sandy Springs to see the action.

And Hump and me. That added up to ten. Not enough, it seemed, for a show.

"You hungry?"

I turned to Hump. "Not that hungry."

He headed for the buffet. When he returned, he was eating a salami-and-cheese sandwich. "Got to get my money's worth."

"You'll need a stomach pump."

"Not me. I'm cast iron."

While he was eating the sandwich, two more men drifted in. They were wearing suits and had name tags on. Probably some convention or other. The bartender, without asking, took them cans of Coke. That done, he moved down the bar and stopped across from Hump and me. "You from out of town?"

"Nope," I said.

"It's a great town." He was moving away when I stopped him. "California?"

"Huh?"

"You from California?"

"Sure." He looked puzzled. "How'd you know?"

"Accent," I said. "I spent some time out there."

"In the service?"

I nodded.

"World War Two?" He'd over-guessed my age. It was a usual thing.

"The Korean one."

"Oh." He moved me down a few years but I was still around fifty in his eyes.

It wasn't one of the world's great conversations. It would have died in ten or twenty more seconds. His eyes eased past me, looking for somebody who needed another soft drink. About that time, the door near the right side of the stage opened and a man walked out. No, it wasn't so much a walk or a stride. It was a TV ad for a man who took the right vitamins in the morning. Every morning.

He wore a dark gray suit, a white shirt and a tie just a shade or two lighter than the suit. He wore silver-rimmed glasses, square framed, and his blocky face looked tanned under some freshly applied talc. This man was management. It was written on him in foot-high letters. And when he stopped at the far end of the bar, the bartender left us and headed toward him at a trot.

There was a laugh at the main entrance. I looked in that direction and saw four men, wearing the same convention name tags, enter. They'd been on the town for some hours. The man who passed close to me had that flushed, glazed look to his face.

The bartender left the management type and offered them Cokes and waved past us at the free-lunch counter. I watched that and I studied the man in the gray suit. His eyes were doing a head count. He finished the tables and he swung his head and faced me. Behind me, Hump straightened up to his full height and stepped away from the bar. He was headed for the buffet counter again. I looked over my shoulder at Hump and said, "Hey, don't push your luck."

"The first one didn't get me."

I shook my head at him and turned away. At the far end of the bar the management man was staring. He seemed to be counting Hump and me more than once. At least he'd had time. When he saw me staring back, he pushed away from the bar. He said something to the bartender and, with the same assured march step, he went through the door next to the stage.

I waved my empty Coke can at the bartender. He brought two more. While he pulled the tabs I said, "Who's that?"

"Where?"

"The man in the gray suit."

"The owner, Mr. Thomlin."

"Owner or manager?"

He shrugged and walked away.

Hump returned with a thick sandwich. I looked at it. "A salami-and-potato-salad sandwich," he said.

The lights came up slowly on the stage. There was the hum of an amplifier. This led to a screech and then one of those deep actor's voices started in.

"The Bird's Nest Revue presents our Bicentennial salute to America. After two hundred years it is still the land of the free and the home of the brave. In the beginning, before the white man came to these shores, there were the Indians."

A loud blare of music. It was the pop recording of "Cherokee Nation." A young black girl, wearing nothing but a beaded headband, did a leap from the wings. She began a dance that was partly go-go and partly the stomp-and-trot parody of a war dance. In the downstage lights, front to the audience, her pubic hair looked like a pad of rusty steel wool.

Hump said, "That ain't no Indian."

After the black Indian there was a Pilgrim girl who danced with a big squash in her hands. A couple of times I thought she was going to do something rude with the vegetable. She didn't and she was followed by the Revolutionary Army girl. She was slim and had dark hair and did a manual of arms with a wooden musket.

The fourth girl, the Dixie girl, was a huge Midwest type with thighs like a draft horse. She wore a Rebel Army cap and did some marching about the small stage with the same wooden musket.

"…and bloody but unbowed, proud of its past and looking forward to the future, the South returned to the Union." A slow and mournful version of "Dixie" underscored the narration.

It began as a feeling. I felt closed in. Like the air was being sucked away by too many lungs. Two men entered the club during the Dixie-girl number. They'd pressed to the bar, right in front of me, between me and the stage. I could smell the Brut on them. It was like they'd splashed each other with about a quart of it. That got me thinking. I looked over my shoulder at Hump and saw that two more men had entered about the same time and they were behind Hump, between him and the buffet counter.

One of the men in front of me at the bar, the nearest one, turned on his elbow and looked at me. The look didn't mean anything. It was a tape measure.

I tapped Hump on the arm. "I'm tired. Let's take a table."

I led the way to the nearest table. I looked back and saw that one of the two near the buffet had left the bar and was walking toward the main entrance. He stopped there and leaned on the cigarette-machine top. At the bar, the other three men edged together until they were shoulder to shoulder. Eyes on us.

"Some show," I said.

Hump looked down at the knuckles of his right hand. "I count six."

"Huh? Four."

"Two at the table behind me," Hump said.

I leaned forward. He was right. Two more at that table. I leaned away and blew out a slow breath. "I should have let you give me that five-minute lecture."

"Late now for that," he said. "I think we ought to make a run for the door. Only one there."

It had been building. I'd noticed it earlier and then the girls had taken my mind off it. Those last three beers and the Cokes were putting on the pressure. I was about to wet my underwear. "I'm floating a kidney."

"Shit."

I located the men's room. It was a door to the left of the stage. I pushed back my chair. "Soon as I walk back you throw a chair at those three at the bar and we make a run."

"If you don't draw flies back there."

It was the risk. It had to take it. I could hardly move. The bladder pain was beginning. "I hope not. Not in my condition." I wagged my way through the jumble of tables. I reached the men's room and didn't look back. I went in. It was empty. There was a wash basin and a mirror and a paper-towel box to the right. On the left there were two metal stalls without doors. I trotted for the nearest stall. I was just starting, just beginning to feel the relief, when I heard the door open behind me. The music was louder and the recorded music playing was "When Johnny Comes Marching Home again."

I looked over my shoulder. The water was running in the wash basin. A squat dark man in a white polo shirt was standing at the mirror. He was combing his hair. It was long greasy hair and he combed it with a flair while his eyes watched me in the mirror.

"Jim Hardman, right?"

I hissed on. Give me five seconds. "Who?"

"Don't play games, smartass."

"I'm not playing games. I'm here to watch the girls."

Finished. Full limp relief. I zipped up. I gave the toilet handle a push.

"You're on the wrong turf," the dark man said.

"Why? Is this a gay joint?"

One step. I didn't want to get caught in the stall. It would be a metal cage. Another step. I was almost clear of the stall. Another step. Then a fist came out of nowhere and blind-sided me. The man who threw it was blind too, blocked by the stall, and the fist hit me on the shoulder and skidded off the bone and struck my cheek. The surprise got me. I hadn't known that second man was there and I could feel myself falling until I slammed against the front edge of the stall. I was half down when a second fist hit me in the chest and drove me into the back part of the cubical. I tried to grab the rim of the toilet bowl but missed and my hand went deep into the water.

There was a crash from the club. Maybe Hump had thrown the chair early. A girl screamed. All hell was breaking out in the main room. The squat dark man had taken a step toward me while he stored away his comb. Now he stepped to the side and nodded at the other man. "Finish it." He moved out of sight and the door opened and closed.

The other man, the one I really hadn't seen, now blocked the stall entrance. He was tall and lean and he had what might be called a dutch-boy cut for his blond hair. He squared his feet and started his move toward me.

I got my hand almost out of the toilet bowl. Then I thought better of it and reached in deeper. I cupped my hand. He was closer. He said, "You heard the man. He said to finish it." I swung my arm and threw the handful of water into his eyes.

Maybe he was fastidious. Maybe he thought there was still piss in the water. Or it might have been just the surprise. He backed away and scrubbed a hand over his face. I scrambled to my feet. The floor was slick from somebody's bad aim. I braced a foot against the toilet bowl and pushed off. I smacked into the lean man and rammed him across the room. My shoulder was under his ribs and when we hit the wall, I think I felt some ribs cave in. The breath went out of him in a loud explosion.

He kicked at me and caught my shin. I swung the wet hand low and hit him in the groin. He didn't have the breath left for a scream. He went limp and dragged at me. I swung him in a dance step and threw him against the stall wall. He hit it with his face and bounced away and hit the floor face down. I stepped around him and kicked him in the face twice. That was to keep him still.

He was still all right. I backed away and took a deep breath. There was another crash and crunch from the club. It was going on out there and that was the only way out. I had another look at the downed man to make certain he was out of it. He was. Then I pushed the door open and went looking for Hump.

CHAPTER TWELVE

The sound was from a tape recorder. The narration and the music were still going on. The stage was empty. The deep actor's voice boomed on. "...the war for the self-determination of a whole people thousands of miles away from our own safe shores..." The music under it sounded like "China Nights" played on two or three guitars.

All the paying customers had left. The front door was closed and the bartender stood there with his back to the door. I wasn't going in that direction anyway. The real action was in the corner of the room next to the door that led backstage.

The club was a wreck. Tables were overturned the whole length of the bar room. One of the hard-asses was on the floor, face down. He wasn't moving and I made my guess that he hadn't seen it coming. One more man leaned against the bar. His face was twisted with pain and he held his right shoulder. It looked broken or dislocated.

The other men, among them the squat dark man who'd been in the men's room, were stalking Hump. Three of them. They'd seen the damage he could do and now they were careful. They were trying to pressure him out of the corner. He wanted the wall at his back.

Hump's breath rasped. It had been going on too long. There was a cut on the right side of his face. His shirt was torn from the pocket down to the hem. The black hard mean was running in him. He was at the point where he didn't give a shit about how much he got hurt if he could give back more of it than he got.

I hadn't gone that far. Not quite. The bad thing about fighting was being afraid you'd get hurt. Then after the first hurts, it didn't matter anymore. I'd taken those licks and my face, the right side of it, was numb. But I wasn't quite there yet.

I started my fat, quiet trot toward the three that had Hump cornered. The one nearest to me was the dude in the white polo shirt. His back was to me. Hump saw me coming. His face didn't show it and when he saw my direction, he took a step toward the dude in the polo shirt and swung at him. That kept him occupied. He ducked and backed away. I was almost on top of him when the bartender, from the front door, yelled, "Watch out, Tim."

The dark man in the polo shirt heard him and whirled. I swung at him and missed and ran belly to belly against him. He fell backward toward Hump. He got within one stumbling step before Hump hit him in the neck and dropped him.

One of the remaining two men faced me. He was a sandy-haired guy in a blue leisure suit. His lip was split and a thread of blood ran down his chin. He swung at me and hit me with a right. I took part of it on my shoulder. The arm felt dead to the fingers. I braced myself for a left.

To my left, Hump backed the other dude up against the bar and hit him three times. They were blows that sounded like somebody thumping the bottom of an empty tin tub. That one went over the bar, head-first.

The left I'd expected didn't come. Blue leisure suit backed away from me and faced Hump. He knew it was over and he was ready to give it up if there was a way. I lunged after him and hit him in the side of the neck with a right that didn't do much damage. But blue leisure suit wanted to pretend that it was enough. He started his dive for the floor. Hump didn't want it to be that easy. Hump caught him by the shoulder and righted him. He brought his knee up, at the same time pulling the man's head down. His face hit Hump's knee and he gurgled and fell away. Hump let him fall. It was over.

"…and that's the Bird's Nest Revue's salute to America. I hope you've enjoyed it. Tell your friends. And now here are the girls one last time …"

The bartender left the front door and crabbed along the wall. He wanted to keep his distance. He didn't want any part of Hump.

Hump spat blood at him. "Cunts," he said.

Behind us, on the stage, the black girl walked out stared out at wreckage. "Where's everybody?"

Hump opened the door and bowed me out. "That was some leak you took."

"You had to be there," I said.

I stood in the doorway to Hump's bathroom. It was his place, so I waited while he washed up and balled up the torn shirt and dropped it in the trash can next to the john. "That's fourteen dollars down the chute."

The numb feeling had left the right side of my face. It was puffy now and I kept pushing at the teeth. Two of them on the low back side seemed to have some give. I'd have trouble eating for a few days. If I was lucky neither of them would fall out during the night.

"Something bothers me," Hump said.

"I know the question." I took off my shirt. I edged past him and ran the hot water and rinsed my face and my arms up to the elbows. The skin on the right side of my jaw felt feverish. I cut off the hot water and ran the cold. I cupped some water in my hand and swished it around my mouth. There was a pale color of blood when I spat.

"You know so much, what's the question?"

I wiped my face with a towel. "You want to know what we were doing at that place. What was the *real* reason?"

Hump leaned in the doorway. "You got an answer?"

"I might have one tomorrow."

"I don't believe this."

I shook my head. I didn't have any words for it. I'd been curious. I'd wanted to see the operation. I'd wanted to see what those California dudes looked like. And, of course, there'd been the girls. None of those would make much sense to Hump.

Hump spread his hands and looked at the puffy backs, the skinned knuckles and the thumb that had swollen to about twice its usual size. "You goddamn crackers."

I tried laughing. It hurt too much.

"I understand you are still working for me."

I took the phone out of my ear and rolled over. I found the lamp switch and fumbled for my watch on the night table.

"You still there, Mr. Hardman?"

I turned the watch. It was five minutes after three in the morning. Or it was five minutes after three in the afternoon. My brain felt like soft scrambled eggs. No, it was morning. I could see the blinds were open a bit and there was darkness beyond them. "The hell you say I'm still working for you."

"That is what people are saying on the street."

"It's a lie. We don't work for you."

"I see. It was the matter of Buck Thomas."

I swung my legs over the edge of the bed and sat up. "I thought we had a deal."

"We did." The Man took his time. He had the hammer and the nail. "But that applied only if you found him. You didn't find him, did you?"

"You know I did."

"It appears that you have an odd idea about the deals you make. You accepted my money, Mr. Hardman."

"You want it back?"

"I understand there was trouble at The Bird's Nest last night."

I said, "It was a mistake."

"Then it was a fortunate mistake. The street word is that you were quite rough on some of their best."

"Not me. That was Hump." I moved the phone to my left ear. I rubbed the right side of my jaw. I had a lump the size of a lemon between my gum and the skin. "You call me for any special reason, Pike?"

"I was having trouble sleeping."

"Take a pill." It wasn't the way I liked to get my information. Call it curiosity if you like. I wanted to know if what he knew tailed with what Baylor and Franklin thought. "Exactly what did Buck Thomas tell you?"

"All he knew," Pike said. "But then, you're not working for me, are you?"

"That's right." I reached out and slammed the receiver on the base. I got as far as the door to the living room before the phone rang again. I let it ring. It was still ringing when I returned to the bedroom with the scotch and rocks I'd mixed in the kitchen. I sat on the edge of the bed and waited. It stopped abruptly in the middle of a ring. I moved the receiver off the hook.

The phone hummed to me while I tried to numb the lump in my jaw. It took two drinks.

I had breakfast late. Nothing that I had to chew. Juice and coffee. After a read at the *Constitution,* I headed for the bathroom and a shower. On the way past the bed, the phone hummed at me. I put the receiver back on the base. I didn't reach the bathroom before it rang.

It was Art Maloney. "I just reported your phone out of order."

"Thanks."

"You going to be there?"

I said I was. I didn't have any plans. I didn't need to look at my watch. "You're working late."

"With reason," he said. "You'll be there in half an hour?"

"In the backyard."

I showered and dressed. It was early for a beer. I had a bit of a headache or the faraway threat of one. I settled for a glass of plain tonic water. I sat on the back steps and sipped the tonic water. The two loose teeth didn't care much for the cold, so I put the glass aside and smelled the green lushness of the yard. I closed my eyes and put my head against the porch door frame. I thought I could smell flowers.

I awoke and found Art seated on the step below me. I didn't know how long he'd been there. He had a plain brown envelope next to his shoe and he was smoking a Pall Mall from the pack I'd brought out with me.

"You look like hell," he said.

"I slipped in the shower."

"Accidents happen." He opened the clasp on the back of the brown envelope and tapped the side of the envelope on the step until several Polaroid color photos fell into his hand.

He passed them to me. I looked at the top one. It was enough. It was a picture of a dead black man. It was taken from enough distance so that I could see that the man was stuffed into the trunk of an automobile. Next to the body of the man, there was a shotgun with the stock broken off.

"Is this somebody I'm supposed to know?" I passed the photos to him.

"I think Buck Thomas knew them."

It figured. It explained the call from The Man. He'd wanted to do his brag that the killers of Smiley Gibbs had been wasted. I hadn't let him. Or he'd backed away from telling me.

"How many?"

"Three of them," Art said.

I lifted my glass. The ice had melted and a couple of bugs had decided to try the tonic water. I poured it out. "Where?"

"The airport."

"That dump heap." It was true. A lot of the gangland people were leaving their garbage at the airport. The car would be parked in one of the distant lots and it would stay there until the meat in the trunk got ripe enough to be noticed. The car would be stolen or it would belong to the dead man.

"Two in one trunk. One in the other."

I went into the kitchen and rinsed out the glass. A couple of ice cubes and the rest of the tonic and I returned to the steps. "I guess they couldn't stuff all three into one trunk. Three shotguns?"

He nodded. "All with busted stocks."

"That Pike is a bastard about details."

"And you're not working for him anymore?"

"Everybody wants an answer to that question. Even Pike. I think I'll hold a press conference later this afternoon. I'll have a press release ready."

"Be ready for some questions about The Bird's Nest on Peachtree."

"Huh?" I gave him my best dumb look.

"I saw a report on a disturbance there last night. One man with a broken shoulder, one with a concussion, others with missing teeth and other bruises."

"You get a description of the army did the damage?"

"That's the odd part. The people at the club didn't want to talk about it. They got pressed and they said a fat black man and a tall white guy about seven feet did it. Seems these two guys were trying to make passes at the girls in the show."

"Well, you know me." I had a swallow of the tonic water. "Marcy won't let me go to girlie shows anymore."

Art let it drop. "I think we'll need to talk to Pike."

"He's among the missing. He calls me again and I'll tell him."

Art shoved the photos in the envelope and closed the clasp. "It's getting rough."

"It'll stop when one side runs out of bodies."

"Call me."

I watched him round the back corner of the house and head for the drive. I went inside and called Marcy at work. I gave her some fairy tale and she called her dentist. She called back to say that the dentist would fit me in on an emergency basis.

About two hours later and about a hundred dollars' poorer I still didn't know if I was going to lose the two teeth.

CHAPTER THIRTEEN

I woke up bloated with cream soups and starving for the taste of something with blood in it.

The call about the dentist had Marcy running over right after work. What I'd wanted was some steak or shrimp or a pork chop. One look at my jaw and Marcy got the mother's pity on her face like she was about to say "Poor baby" and drove away again. A quarter of an hour later, she was back with a half-dozen cans of cream soups. Cream of chicken, cream of mushroom, cream of tomato, green pea and asparagus. All those. And a gallon of milk.

I guess I'd shaken her out of her sad funk. That pleased me so much, I let her warm a can of mushroom for me. I drank it out of a cup with the proper amount of appreciation. Then we watched one of the educational TV channels for a couple of hours. One program was about bugs and worms that live underground. The second one was about an old black jazz piano player. During one of the station breaks, Marcy heard my stomach rumble and made me another cup of soup, this time cream of tomato, and I drank that one too.

I think she wanted to stay the night. I believe she couldn't decide if kissing me would hurt my jaw. She sat there struggling with it for a time and she left at midnight, forlorn, looking like a nurse who'd just been laid off. I stayed up another hour and watched part of a tape of the Reds and Braves game that had been televised earlier while I'd been learning about bugs and worms and whorehouse piano.

So I was starving the next morning. I scrambled a couple of eggs. I passed up the bacon but I wanted toast. I didn't have trouble with the eggs but the toast had my jaw screaming at me.

I was about done with breakfast when I heard the thump on the front door. It didn't have the sound of knuckles. Odd. It made me wonder if kudzu had overgrown the doorbell. I hitched up my boxer shorts and headed for the door. I got there in time for the second thump.

"Yeah?"

"Paper boy collecting." The voice was easy to recognize. It was hoarse and raspy.

I opened the door and nodded Baylor, the Intelligence cop, inside. He was alone. "You moonlighting?"

He passed me the morning paper he'd used to thump my door. "Not yet."

"Where's your shadow?"

"Franklin's under the weather."

He followed me into the kitchen. I lit the burner under the kettle and spooned some instant into a clean cup. I sat down and peeled the rubber band from the *Constitution*. I ran my eyes over the headline stories on page one. Baylor watched me. He loosened his tie and stood by the stove until the water was hot enough. He mixed his own cup and brought it to the table.

"You're reading the wrong page," he said.

"Which one is the right one?"

"Page four, the left side of the page."

I turned the pages. I found it without any trouble. The headline caught me. *Gangland Killing*. I read the short paragraph. It concerned the shotgun killing of a Robert (Bobby) Biddoux. He was a reputed gambling figure with a number of arrests in the last few years. The story wasn't complete. It looked like the story had come in late and they didn't have all the details yet.

"It was the flyby in the parking lot this time," Baylor said.

"Biddoux?" The name picked at me. I had the feeling I'd heard or seen the name in the last few days.

"He ran the bug for Pike," Baylor explained.

"Ah, *that* Bobby Biddoux." He'd been on the list The Man had given me that night at his place, that he'd let me memorize and then he'd burned. We'd never got past the first name on the list, Smiley Gibbs.

I refolded the front section and dropped it in the empty chair next to me. I moved to the sports section. The Reds had won 7 to 4 the night before. That satisfied my curiosity. I hadn't stayed with the game long enough to see the final totals.

"I talked to Matt Turlow this morning."

"That right?" I kept the interest down. I didn't want to bubble. "Officially?"

He shook his head.

"What does Turlow say?"

"He's talking good sense. He doesn't want the bloodbath either. He's ready to talk to Pike."

"I bet he is."

"He means it. He knows this is a dead-end street they're on."

"He took the first step," I said. "Remember P. J. Turner?"

"My problem is that I can't reach Pike."

"That's probably the way he wants it. Pike wants to talk to you he'll let you know about it."

"I've put the word on the street."

"He'll hear it then."

"Without the strong argument I've got," Baylor said.

"What Pike is hearing is what happened last night. The flyby on his boy, Biddoux. It's going to make the rest of his hearing all screwed up." I didn't need this early-morning visit. I couldn't concentrate on the sports section. The last part of my egg was cold. My house was turning into a Grand Central of cops on their way to other parts of town.

"Reach Pike for me."

"It's not that easy."

"Think of it as self-interest." Baylor sipped his coffee and watched me over the rim of the cup. I waited. "Turlow's hot for your body. He gets the word you've quit working for Pike. Next thing he knows, you and Evans come in and wreck his place. Just showing up at The Bird's Nest was enough. That was why he puts six of his best on you."

"Wait a minute. You say Turlow put those six on us?"

Baylor dipped his head. "He recognized you. Of course, Evans being with you helped with the ID"

"Wait a minute." My head wasn't working well. It was too early in the day. "Describe him for me."

The word picture fitted the man the bartender at The Bird's Nest had said was Mr. Thomblin, the owner. It was right down to the silver-rimmed glasses. The last I'd seen of him was when he'd gone in the stage-door entrance to the right of the stage. To make his phone calls that brought the six hard-asses pounding over to stomp on Hump and me.

"And he's mad?"

"Burning, steaming, stinking mad," Baylor said.

I dropped the sports page in the same chair seat with the front section. I went into the bedroom and closed the door behind me. I found the list of four phone numbers The Man had given me the night he'd dropped by. The phone on my knee, I called the first number on the list, the one marked for six a.m. to noon. I let the phone ring about a dozen times. No answer. Without stopping, except for the dozen rings on each of them, I ran through the list. Nothing.

Back in the kitchen. I dropped the list on the table in front of Baylor.

"What's this?"

"Proof I can't reach him." I explained the four numbers. "I think they're all pay phones."

"Nobody home?"

"I think he's changed the locations and the phones."

He pushed back his chair. "In the bedroom?"

I nodded. He went off and I cleared the kitchen table. All but the coffee cups. I was still hungry. A step away from another stomach rumble.

The bedroom door was open. I walked in. Baylor stood over the night table, reading the phone numbers from the list into the phone mouthpiece. I got shorts and a T-shirt out of the bureau and went into the bathroom and shaved and showered. It took me about ten minutes. When I came out, he wasn't in the bedroom anymore. I finished dressing and joined him in the kitchen.

He looked up from a second cup of coffee. "They're all pay phones." He waited until I was seated and pushed the list toward me. Beside each number he'd scribbled a location, an address, for each phone. It looked like the four points of the compass.

I put a crease next to the address beside the midnight-to-six-a.m. number. "This mean anything to you?"

He shook his head.

"If I know that area, that phone booth is two or three blocks from the warehouse where you found Buck Thomas's body."

"That means something?"

"I'm not sure." I looked at the list again. "But if you're not doing anything the rest of the morning … ?"

"It's wide open."

I got a jacket from the bedroom closet. I didn't bother with a tie. We went out and got in his unmarked car. I settled in and watched him back out of my drive. "And Matt Turlow is mad at me?"

"He wants your hide pegged to the wall."

"And if I put you in touch with Pike, he'll forgive me?"

"Something like that," Baylor said.

Dumb crap. That's dump crap.

The pay phone was on the shady side of a shop that specialized in locks, deadbolts and home safety alarms. They were, if you went by the number of trucks they had, doing a booming business. The special this week was a smoke-and-fire detection device.

Baylor waited in the car. I went into the booth and checked the number on the face of the phone. It matched. I came out and looked around. There was a metal bumper rail and parking spaces for four or five cars next to the phone booth.

I got back in the car. Baylor stared at me for a few seconds. He wasn't sure what this was all about. I couldn't tell him because I was playing the part of the hunch that was in the sunlight. The other part was in the dark.

"This a snipe hunt, Hardman?"

"Maybe." I nodded at the street. "Loop the block one time."

He made it a slow drive, a box step. At the end of it, I didn't know any more than I had at the beginning. I didn't want to admit it. I pointed east. "Loop the next block."

We did that one. Still nothing. At the end of it, we were back in the area near the lock shop. I aimed a finger at the block on the west side of the shop. "Do that one."

It was a different kind of area we drove through. The block to the east had been residential. The block to the west seemed to be the beginning of a commercial zone. Or it had been at one time. Now it appeared to be part of the economic blight that had hit parts of Atlanta.

On the far side of this block there was a low and wide brick building. The flaking Coca-Cola sign over the main entrance had "James Body Shop" on it. It was a deserted building.

"Here," I said.

Baylor pulled to the curb. "Here what?"

"You get to show me how well you can break and enter."

Baylor found a window at the rear of the building. It was next to a large parking lot. The out back area hadn't been paved. It was dirt and gravel and now some weeds, waist high, had rooted themselves there. Besides the window that wasn't locked, there was a locked door and one of those huge roll-up doors that was wide and high enough so that a moving van could drive in without trouble.

Baylor almost split the seat of his pants getting through the window. I waited outside until he unlocked the small door from the inside.

Inside, there was the smell of old gas and oil. The dust scent wasn't that strong. My guess was that the body shop hadn't been out of business more than six months or so.

I walked past Baylor. It was mainly one big room. Near the front there were some closed-in spaces that might have been offices at one time. A ramp passed those spaces. It led to the main entrance way, a low-ceilinged doorway that must have been intended for cars only. "See if the power's on," I said.

Baylor tried a wall switch. Nothing. He went the length of the shop and entered one of the officelike spaces. I heard some thuck-thuck sounds and the overhead lights went on. I guess he'd found the main power switches.

I went to the roll-up back door. There was a switch there and I could see the motors up high. I hit the switch and the door began its smooth upward movement. I hit the switch and reversed it. It settled downward again.

Baylor stuck his head out of the office space. "Need the power anymore?"

"Cut it."

He did. The overhead lights went off. I waited until he was beside me. Then I pointed down at the tire tracks in the thin layer of dust on the shop floor. "You get it yet?"

"No." He squatted and stared at the treads.

"The last time I saw Pike he said he wasn't going to be at his apartment, that he was going to be moving around." I touched the tire tracks with the toe of my shoe. "I didn't know he meant it literally."

"In what?" He straightened up.

"At that warehouse, the one where Buck Thomas was, you notice the tire tracks and the oil drippings?"

"Sure. It was some truck they hauled Buck Thomas there in."

I shook my head at him. "Wouldn't need a truck."

"Then … what … ?"

I walked a few paces toward the center of the shop, away from the motorized door. "Here." I waited for him to stand next to me. "See those?" They were single tires. When he nodded, I led him to a space near the roll-up door. "See any difference?"

Baylor shook his head.

"Wider here," I said. "Looks like double width. Two tires on each side here."

"All right." He nodded. I could see that he was still puzzled.

"What has single tires on the front and double tires on the back?"

"You tell me."

"Some kinds of trucks. But also some kinds of mobile homes." I walked away from him. I headed for the door that led into the back parking area. I stopped in the doorway. "My guess is a mobile home of one sort or the other. The self-contained type. The cab and home part as one unit." I stepped out of the doorway. He closed the door and locked it. I walked across to the open window and waited there for him. I caught his arm so he wouldn't fall when his foot didn't quite clear the side of the window frame.

He grunted his thanks. I watched while he brushed the knees of his slacks. "We know all this, what does it tell us?"

"That he doesn't trust hotels and motels?"

"Funny," he said.

"No, I mean it. This way he's got most of the comforts of home and he's juking and jiving around town. Six hours here and then a drive over to the next place. Six hours there. Each place he's got power and all he does is roll out the extension cord.

Lights and maybe air-conditioning if he needs it and electricity for his stove and refrigerator. And no bellhop or night clerk can sell his ass for a hundred dollars."

"You're a lot of help, Hardman."

We walked around the side of the building. We reached Baylor's Plymouth.

"But the other night, to get that information from Buck Thomas, he dumped in his nest. There went that location, the warehouse." I looked at my watch. It was still half an hour until noon. I waved a hand at the body shop. "If I understand his setup, he ought to be in there right now, until noon. He's not. I think he picked himself four more holes to hide in."

"And four more pay phones nearby?"

"That's it." I walked around the Plymouth and got in the passenger side.

"How do I find him?"

"You stop every mobile home that's driven by a black."

He started the engine. "It's that easy?"

"Nobody said it was supposed to be easy."

He wanted me to go with him and look for the other two locations. I begged off. That was the real snipe hunt. A waste of time. He dropped me at my house. I went in and fought off a stomach growl with a can of pea soup.

I didn't even allow myself an oyster cracker.

CHAPTER FOURTEEN

S uppertime. Hump called and when he found that Marcy was
with me, he surprised us by dropping by with three steaks. It
was, he thought, time for a cookout. He didn't know that Marcy
still had me on soup until she wrapped one of the steaks in foil
and stored it in the freezer. I could have it in a few days.

If that was the way it was going to be, I wasn't going to do the
cooking. I sat on the steps with a beer and watched while Hump
did it all wrong. He didn't stack the charcoal and he didn't soak
it in the fluid before he lit it.

To keep from instructing him in the right way, I told him
about the visit from Baylor and what I'd discovered about
Warden Pike's moving motel room.

"That's easy."

"What is?"

"A guess I've got." He handed me the tongs on the way past,
on the way into the house. "Keep an eye on things for me."

The door closed behind him. I went to the grill and, using
the tongs, I stacked the charcoal so that air could pass under and
around the single briquets. I was done with that when Marcy
came to the porch doorway and asked if I wanted anything.

"A cup of warm blood."

She handed me a Bud instead. Some nurse. "You sure this
isn't bad for me?"

"It's got green vitamins in it."

Smart girl. She'd finished making the salad and washing and
wrapping the potatoes. She placed the potatoes on the step below

her and sat down hip-to-hip with me. There was a look on her face that said she thought I might break down and cry. She was right. When the coals got right and the steak juices starting dripping and hissing and the meat smell filled the backyard, I might very well cry.

I rubbed the side of my face. The swelling had gone down some. The lump was there still. It felt about the size of a walnut.

Hump stepped over me. He took the tongs. "Remember me telling you about Johnny Cott?"

I shook my head.

"At the contest the other night? When Smiley Gibbs got killed?"

I remembered. He'd got Hump's vote and Hump got one of his girls.

"He plays a bit. Maybe a bit too much. He keeps those girls hustling to keep him in chips."

"What's that got to do with … ?"

"Patience," Hump said. He turned and looked at the grill. He saw that I'd stacked the briquets and, for a second, I thought he'd knock them apart. He didn't. Maybe he liked my design instinct. "Some months back, back around the first of the year, he invited me to sit in on a game. It was about the time the papers were filled with a police crackdown. Raids on some hotel rooms where games were going on. I told him I didn't see myself spending the night in the slammer for the privilege of giving those dudes my cash."

Marcy leaned closer to me. Her head dropped on my shoulder. There was some soreness there. A fist had bounced off before it hit me in the side of my face. I didn't move. The warmth was for me, even though her attention was with Hump.

"Johnny Cott almost laughed himself into a strangling fit. The way he told it Jack Tyrone, who handles gambling for The Man …"

"He was on the list?"

Hump nodded. "Well, this Tyrone had worked out something. He'd bought himself a mobile home or maybe he'd taken it to settle losses in a game. Anyway, whichever, Tyrone fixed that mobile home with a poker table, an extra big refrig and a bar. The game would start at ten. They meet in some parking lot. Everybody'd park their cars and get into the mobile home. He would drive the mobile home somewhere and park it. Maybe in some deserted building. A garage, a warehouse. The game would break up about six or seven. The mobile home would pull into the parking lot and the players would step out, get into their cars and drive off."

"What was the call you made?"

"I called Cott. I asked about the game. He said it wasn't going and it hadn't for better than a week. The story he got was that the rig was in the shop for repairs."

"For better than a week?"

"I asked him that. He said he understood they had to order some parts."

"A kingsize bed for Pike," I said.

"Likely."

"That Pike's got class. Matt Turlow is tearing up the town looking for him. His soldiers asking and buying people. Checking the hotels and motels, apartment house, and all this time Pike's riding around in his kingsize bed. He changes locations every six hours and he's probably not using a location but two or three days."

"Running his empire with a pocketful of dimes for the pay phones. Got to admire a man like that."

Marcy lifted her head from my shoulder. "Is that all of the story?"

"Yes."

"It's not one of your better ones." Marcy picked up the foil-wrapped potatoes and carried them to the grill. She dropped them on the coals. Smash. There went my careful stacks and pyramids.

I told myself it wasn't my concern. What ought to concern me was the kind of soup left in the pantry. I think there was cream of chicken, cream of asparagus and the last can of cream of tomato.

I heated my cup of cream of tomato and took it into the living room and watched the CBS News while Hump and Marcy argued about whether the steaks had been on the grill long enough or too long. The bickering bothered me almost as much as the smell of the cooking meat. Almost but not quite.

I was staring down at the bottom of my cup when the phone rang. It was Baylor.

"Yeah?"

"Checking to see if you've heard from Pike."

"Not yet."

"I'm afraid there'll be a payback from him sometime tonight unless we reach him."

"Blessed are the peacemakers."

He ignored that. "You'll call me?"

I said I would.

I carried my empty cup into the kitchen. The fussing was over. Marcy and Hump were seated across the table from each other. Good hot salty blood ran around the edges of their plate while they hacked and chewed.

I leaned on the back of Marcy's chair and barked. "Scraps anyone?"

It was the doorbell. It took me a few seconds of listening to the hum of the phone to realize that. I eased to the edge of the bed and stepped out. Marcy rolled toward me. I put out a hand and touched her and she was still again.

I reached the front door without cutting on the lights and without losing a toe or a kneecap. "Who is it?"

"Man wants to see you."

I unlocked the door. "Come on in." I turned toward the bedroom. I was wearing only my boxer shorts. I wanted at least some trousers and a T-shirt. The door opened behind me. One of The Man's bodyguards stepped in. I recognized him from the last visit. He was Ray, the one who'd wanted to take my piece from me.

"He says come out," Ray said.

"As soon as I put on …"

He caught my arm and swung me toward the open door. Another black caught my other arm there and they pulled me down the steps and across the lawn to the drive. A black LTD was parked there. Just before we reached it the back door swung open. In the brief flash of light, I could see that it was Pike.

He edged toward the far side of the seat. Ray and the other black gave me a shove and slammed the door behind me. The door missed my bare left foot by inches.

"It was nice of you to come out so promptly."

I let out a hiss of breath and tugged at my shorts. "It's hard to refuse those engraved invitations." I looked out the car window. Ray stood next to the door. The other black had moved down the drive until he had stationed himself near the street. "That Ray dude is beginning to get on my nerves."

"Good help is hard to find," Pike said.

"Now that we've discussed the servant problem …"

"You've been snooping."

"That's quite a deal you've got going," I said. "The mobile home."

"You figured that out?"

"It wasn't that hard."

"I find I am puzzled," Pike said. "First you were working for me and then you weren't working for me."

"Got a smoke?"

He passed a package to me. I got out one and he lit it with a slim gold lighter.

"What puzzles me is that you still seem to be working. If you're not working for me, who are you working for?"

"Nobody. I'm the curious type."

"That is dangerous."

"Do me a folk proverb," I said.

"I can do more than that. I can tell Ray you don't like him."

"I wouldn't want to hurt his feelings. He's so sensitive." The smoke was raw on the back of my throat. All that dumb talking. I could feel my head coming together. I was about awake. "Baylor, the cop from Intelligence, was the one who shortcut P. J. Turner and sent him back to Detroit."

"What about him?"

"He's been trying to reach you." I fumbled my way through it. Baylor and his talk with Matt Turlow. The fact that Turlow said he wanted to call it off. That he wanted a truce.

"You believe him?"

"I didn't talk to Turlow. Baylor talked to him. It's Baylor who seems to believe him."

"Why is Baylor in this?"

"Less bodies to shovel off the streets."

He took his time. My eyes were used to the darkness now. I could see his face, the hard lines of it. "I find this hard to believe."

"I can't swear it's for real," I said. I found the ashtray and stubbed out the smoke.

"Maybe this is exactly what I need."

"What?"

"Your belief in the offer. I think I will need your impression."

"Of what?"

"I need to know if you believe Turlow."

"How do I arrange that?"

"You talk to Matt Turlow," Pike said.

"The shit you say. That man wants a pound of my ass."

"Then you will be very careful. It will be in your interest to judge well the validity of the offer."

"You trust me to do that?"

"It will not be complete trust." He paused. He selected his words. "Still, I think you have some out-moded sense of your word and … your honor."

"Thanks." I put a dry edge to it. "Maybe I need to know what's in it for you, Pike."

"You have to know whether I can be trusted?"

"I don't like being in the middle. I set up the meet and Turlow is honest and you aren't, that could get me burned."

"It is a matter of business. I think you can understand that aspect. Between us, not to be repeated, my gross is down almost thirty percent since this began."

I nodded. For Pike, the way I saw him, money meant more than blood.

"You'll see Turlow?"

"I'll try." I said.

Pike reached past me and tapped on the window. His boy, Ray, opened the door.

"Wait a minute. How do I reach you?"

"You won't. I'll reach you."

I got out and stood in the dew. The grass was slick. Ray closed the door. He got into the driver's seat. He backed down the drive. At the head of the drive the other gun got into the seat next to Ray. The LTD pulled away.

I went into the house. In the kitchen I checked the clock. It was 3:45. I was wide awake. I ran some water until it was warm and I wet some paper towels and sat at the table and wiped the dew and the dirt and the grass from my feet.

I found a part of a bottle of calvados in the cabinet. I had a couple of drinks. Then it was four o'clock.

I heard the morning paper thump against the porch. I went back to bed and slept until seven when Marcy got up. Then I found Baylor's home number. He was asleep and his wife didn't want to wake him. I insisted.

He called back in twenty minutes. It was set up.

I went into the kitchen and made myself a cup of instant. I sipped it and thought about how eager Baylor was. I don't remember, during my days on the force, being that way at all.

CHAPTER FIFTEEN

Either Matt Turlow didn't have much class or he was hiding out. I hesitated when Baylor and Franklin, one pace ahead of me, swung off the sidewalk and walked into The Love Bureau. It was a storefront outfit. The signs outside were gaudy, in pinks and purples, and they advertised sexy women and love wrestling and private rooms and the full satisfaction of all kinds of manly fantasies.

The door was wide open. Two girls, one black and one blonde, were seated on the sofa that faced the door. Both girls wore bikini bottoms and see-through tops. The blonde girl had her legs crossed at the knees and she was rocking her right leg. Leg rocking has always been one of my sexual fantasies and I stopped in the doorway and stared at her.

It was a long, narrow room. It was like a stage set. A painting of a full-masted ship was over the sofa. Off to one side there was a tank with about a dozen goldfish in it.

There were two doors. One to the far left, one just to the right of the sofa. Over the door to the left there was a sign: NO SEXUAL CONTACT ALLOWED.

The blonde girl, sill rocking her leg, started to go into her act and her pitch. She recognized Baylor before she got past a smile and some broad lip-licking.

Lip-licking is not one of my sexual fantasies.

"Oh, it's you?"

"That's right, sweetheart."

The blonde shrugged and reached under the sofa arm. I moved to the side and saw that there was a button under there.

She pressed it a time or two. On the other side of the sofa, the black girl reached down and scratched her crotch. She saw me watching and smiled. She had a tooth missing top front.

The blonde rocked on. "When you coming by yourself for some love wrestling?"

"I'd pin you in half a second," Baylor said. He didn't sound interested.

"Ain't that the idea?" the blonde said.

The door to the right of the sofa opened. Beyond it there was a narrow hall. At the end there was a staircase going up. I followed Baylor and Franklin in. I had to turn to the side to pass the man who'd opened the door. On the way by I realized it was the dark-skinned man who'd followed me into the bathroom at The Bird's Nest. His greasy hair was shorter now and there was a bandage on the back of his head. "You, huh, fat man?"

I didn't pay any attention to him. There was another man at the foot of the staircase. He hadn't been at the fight. He looked too well dressed and too civilized for anything like that. He wore a good summer-weight tan suit and a tie that hadn't come from Tie City. And his shoes were polished. It looked like he was the class of the place. He stopped us at the foot of the stairs.

"You'll have to leave your weapons here, gentlemen." He nodded at the greasehead behind us. "Tim will keep them for you."

Baylor shook his head. "I don't leave my piece with anybody."

Franklin didn't move. He stared at the man.

I waited. I knew something. I wanted to see what Baylor would do.

"Then you won't be able to go upstairs," the man said.

Baylor laughed and lifted the edge of his suit jacket. He turned slowly so the man could get a good look. "We're not carrying," Baylor said.

I understood the bit in the parking lot. Before we'd headed for the street both Baylor and Franklin had unclipped their holsters and pieces and locked them away in the trunk of the car.

"You?"

Franklin lifted his coat.

Tim, the man with the grease head, patted me down from my armpits to my shoe tops. When he finished, I turned and looked at him. His eyes were hooded. A curl to his mouth. I decided he didn't like me very much.

The inner office didn't impress me either. It appeared makeshift, like it had been collected from some army-surplus sale. The desk that filled most of the office was wood. It had been banged and scarred. The chairs were metal, the folding type.

Matt Turlow, when we entered, was turned in his chair, looking out the single window. Below the window was a parking lot and beyond that, in the distance, was the Baptist church that had been raising all the hell about what was happening to the neighborhood. It wasn't much of a view.

"Have a chair, Mr. Hardman."

Matt Turlow turned and put his elbows on the desk top. There was nothing on the desk except a pack of Winstons and a book of matches. No phone. No business papers.

I studied the blocky face. The square chin. The silver-rimmed glasses and the flecks of gray in the neat dark hair. Then he took off the glasses and cleaned them with the handkerchief from his breast pocket. Without the glasses, the face didn't seem as strong. He had what looked like pink rabbit eyes and he blinked as he stared at me.

I took the chair he'd indicated. It was to the right of the front of the desk. I looked around the office, at the bare walls, the minimum furnishings. "Maybe my daddy was right. Maybe crime doesn't pay."

"It pays quite well," Turlow said. "I won't argue the crime aspects of this. As a business, it is quite lucrative."

I was surprised at the voice. He sounded like a radio announcer. The full, deep resonance. It was the kind of voice I disliked. The voice as a musical instrument. With radio people

it got to the absurd, to the point where they could read two minutes of news without making a bit of sense. Then I realized I'd
heard that voice before. It was the narrator's voice on the tape
that introduced the girls at The Bird's Nest revue.

"And this is not my office, if that is what you mean. When
you leave here today, I will leave also. It might be too much temp-
tation for your Mr. Pike."

"He doesn't belong to me."

"Then, perhaps, it is more accurate to say that you belong
to him."

I shook my head. "That's not accurate either." And I was
thinking, Jesus Christ, here are two thugs and they're fighting
over the control of the city and both of them talk like they've
spent half their lives taking elocution lessons. What the hell has
crime come to anyway?

Turlow was tired of that. "At any rate, it would be accurate to
assume that you can reach Mr. Pike?"

He seemed hooked on *accurate*. I decided to offer him
another word. "That's not true either."

Turlow looked past me. I knew he was questioning Baylor.
"It's not true?"

There. He'd gotten off *accurate*.

"He can get in touch with me. And he will. Later today."

"I see."

"If I knew where Pike was, I'd be a fool to walk in here. It
might tempt some of you to break a few of my fingers. Then I
couldn't play Chopin on my piano."

"You might be lying." That was the man in the suit who'd
met us at the stairs. Now he stood with his back to the door. Tim,
the other thug, and Franklin had remained below.

"You can always break a few fingers and find out."

It wasn't going anywhere. Baylor moved in until he was
against the front of the desk. "I promised Hardman it wouldn't
get rough. I'd like to keep that promise."

It was a nice gesture. He hadn't made any such promise.

"Certainly." Turlow shook his head at the man at the door. "I think we might be forgetting the purpose of this talk."

"Yes, Mr. Turlow." He settled back against the door.

Turlow adjusted his glasses. There, he was strong again. He began his pitch. Lord, he was long-winded. It was the speech of a man who liked to hear himself talk. It went something like this: There had been a few mistakes the last few days. Perhaps he'd over-reached himself by a few feet. He'd accept the responsibility for many of the mistakes. Other men, no longer working for him, had reacted too quickly, without checking with him. That was behind him, as far as he was concerned. The central point was that all this violence was bad for business. It created a flux. Nothing was sure anymore. He moved on to the profit motive. He danced on that for a time.

So, all things considered, he wanted to back away from this confrontation if it would be done with honor.

I almost flinched when he said *honor.*

He went on. He would back away. There would be no more trouble. He and Pike would coexist in the same sense that Russia and the United States did. Pike could go on with his drugs, the girls, the "bug" and the other gambling. He, Turlow, would go back to operating the girl shows, the bathhouses and the high-class girls who worked the better hotels. That was, he thought, an equal split. Did I think that Mr. Pike would agree to such an arrangement? Would Pike be willing to meet and talk about it?

Turlow was persuasive. I'll say that for him. If he'd been running for public office, I might have voted for him. I didn't expect much out of politicians anyway.

All that performance aside, I had to play devil's advocate. I had to ask the question that The Man would ask of me. "One question?"

"Yes, Mr. Hardman?"

"Why do you need a meeting with Pike? I can pass what you've said on to him. He can agree or disagree and pass that back to me and I can contact Baylor and … ?"

He shook his head slowly, sadly, at me like I was the dumb child. The one who never learned to add past ten. "You've answered your own question. A face-to-face meeting with Pike would iron out all the problems. I could see whether I could trust him and if I believed him all I'd need would be his word and a handshake."

It was weak, very weak. Now he wanted to believe in honor among thieves and killers and pimps and all that.

"We could dispense with messengers and go-betweens."

He pointed that at me. Perhaps Baylor had told him how reluctant I'd been.

I stood. I did it easy. There wasn't any reason to scare anybody into a heart attack. "All I can do is pass it on to him. I can't say how he'll react."

"The meeting place would have to be agreeable to both parties."

I nodded.

"But this is an open meeting. I'd be glad to meet him in Central City Park if that's what he wanted."

Central City Park wasn't that bad an idea. That was a one-block park near Five Points. One of the Coca-Cola people had donated several million dollars to buy the land and turn it into a park. It was fairly new, it was wide open. There was some grass, a few small trees struggling against the pollution, and it was usually pretty crowded by students from nearby Georgia State, by winos and by freaks of all kinds. It wasn't a likely hit location.

"And no tricks?" I said.

"Of course not."

"You pull a trick and it could be hard on me. Pike is not very trusting. He might think I'd had some part in setting him up."

"It will be a business meeting. Nothing more and nothing less."

I headed for the door. The man in the suit got word from Turlow in time to step aside. I went out and down. Baylor followed me. The office door closed behind us. Franklin and Tim were standing fairly far apart. I had a feeling they didn't like each other and there hadn't been much casual conversation between them while they waited for us.

Baylor stopped at the bottom step. He looked back up the stairs. "Bernie," he said to Franklin, "you drive Hardman home and come back for me." He pulled back his sleeve and checked his watch. "I'll be out front in forty minutes."

"Some problem?" Franklin moved over to stand beside me.

"A couple of points I'd better get straight with Turlow." Baylor nodded toward me. "I want to be sure I'm not part of a setup either."

"All right." Franklin checked his watch.

Baylor went up the stairs and knocked at the door. It hadn't opened by the time we left the hallway.

The blonde girl followed us to the sidewalk. "Tell 'em where you got it." It was the Vegas dealer's shout.

"Not me," I said. "I'll just take my shots and hope it goes away."

The blonde howled. It wasn't that funny.

Bernie Franklin drove me home. He was quiet. It wasn't the way he'd been the time or two I'd seen him before. Maybe there was something I didn't know about.

"Baylor said you were under the weather yesterday."

"Just a cold. It's about straightened out."

"Something else bothering you? That deal back there?"

"No." He gave me his innocent look. "What makes you ask?"

I shook my head at him. A feeling. And like all those feelings, part of the time you were wrong.

He dropped me in my driveway. I went in and waited for the phone call. I was still waiting almost an hour later when he returned with Baylor. They settled down in my living room for the wait.

Pike didn't call until a bit after two in the afternoon.

CHAPTER SIXTEEN

At ten after two, Baylor pushed the bedroom door open and walked in. He stood at the foot of the bed and waited. Past him I could see his partner, Franklin. Both of them were into my booze. Baylor carried a scotch and rocks. Franklin had tonic water mixed with something.

"If you're done with him," Baylor said, "I want to talk to him."

I was done. At least I hoped I was. I'd told it pretty straight. What Turlow had said. What I'd said. My impressions of Turlow. Still, there was no way I could promise Warden Pike that it was an up-and-up situation. My daddy had raised few reckless children. In fact, I was an only child.

"Baylor's here. He's the cop I told you about. He wants a few words."

"Put him on," Pike said.

I passed the phone to Baylor. I scooped my smokes from the night table. I'd had enough. Too much. I heard Baylor say, "Mr. Pike, I think I can promise…" and then I pulled the door closed after me. There wasn't any more I wanted to hear. Bernie Franklin wasn't in the living room. I looked in the kitchen. Not there either. There was a fresh bottle of tonic on the kitchen counter. He hadn't replaced the seal cap. Dumb. I mixed myself a rum-and-tonic with a squeeze of lime.

Franklin was up the long slope near the wall that fronts the terrace where I sometimes plant my garden. As I approached him, he lifted his glass in a kind of salute. "Hope you don't mind."

I shrugged. "No problem."

TE LAST OF THE ARMAGEDDON WARS

"Where's Bill?"

That threw me off stride. I realized it was the first time I'd heard Baylor's first name. "On the phone."

"With Pike?"

I nodded.

"You trust Pike?"

"About as much as I trust Turlow." I leaned my butt against the wall and looked at the back of the house. It needed painting and the gutters and the downspouts needed replacing.

"How much is that?"

"About as far as I can throw the Peachtree Plaza Hotel."

"That far?"

"About that far," I said, "give or take an inch or two."

"Bill acts like he believes it."

"It's his dime. He can buy what he wants with it."

I felt his stare. He was trying to read all the way through my eyes into my head. I thought about sweetbreads. I thought about watercress in salads. If he read my mind that ought to confuse him.

He gave up. He turned a hip and looked past the garden plot toward the fence that divides my property from the one directly behind. There were a couple of mourning doves on the top wire of the fence. The doves wanted to scratch around in my garden. Our talk disturbed them and they were waiting for us to leave.

Baylor came down the back steps. He stopped at the base of the slope. "You ready, Bernie?"

Franklin took a long drink and looked at the glass.

"Leave it here," I said.

He said thanks and went down the slope. I pushed away from the wall. "You set it up, Baylor?"

"I think so."

"When and where?"

"You wanted out of it, didn't you?"

"Yeah."

"You're out of it," Baylor said. He put a hand on Franklin's shoulder and turned him. Bernie waved back at me and they walked past the corner of the house. A minute later the engine of the Plymouth started up.

I took my time over my drink. The two mourning doves, just about tame anyway, didn't seem worried about me. They fluttered down into the garden plot and began pecking, picking about. I guess they're just about my favorite birds. That beautiful gray body with the black specks on it, that tiny head, the sound the wings made when they flew and the white fan of their tail feathers.

After fifteen minutes, I went into the kitchen and took out the steak Marcy had frozen the night before. I placed it on the kitchen table and made myself a second drink.

Several times during the evening, later in bed just before I dropped off to sleep, I wondered about the truce meeting. I even watched the late news at 11:30. There were no reports of a bloodbath, no newsreel footage of bodies being carted away.

It had, I guessed, been a friendly affair.

It was 10:30 the next morning before I found out that it wasn't that easy. I was on the back steps drinking about my tenth cup of coffee when I heard the front doorbell. I walked around the side of the house and found Bernie Franklin on my front steps. He'd given up on the doorbell and was using the palm of his hand on the door.

"I'm out back."

He followed me. He caught me at the end of the drive, where it touches the garage. He matched steps with me. I had a sideways glance at him. He was sweating. It wasn't that hot. It was cool and breezy.

"A coffee, Bernie?"

He looked at his watch. "A quick one."

"That's the only kind I've got."

"Black."

I made him the coffee and brought it to the back steps. He was seated on the low step. I sat down above him and to his left.

"Thanks."

"Problems?"

His hand shook. He lifted the other hand and used both hands to steady the cup. When he lowered it there was a dribble of coffee on his chin. "Who said there was a problem?"

"If there's not a problem, what the fuck are you doing in my yard?"

"I don't know if I can trust you."

"All this talk about trust bores the shit out of me." I lit a smoke and blew the clouds at him. "I had enough of it yesterday."

"Art said I could trust you."

"You trust Art?" Now it was a word game. I didn't know why he was wasting my time.

"Yes."

"Then go over and talk to Art."

"I can't. He's department."

I placed my smoke on the step and had a sip of my coffee. "I'm not department. That mean you can talk to me?"

"It's not that easy."

The coffee was cold. I threw the dregs into the yard and stood. "I'm going in and make myself a fresh cup. By the time I come back, you make up your mind or get the fuck out of my yard." I took my time in the kitchen. I put in fresh water. I let it heat to a rolling boil. I mixed the coffee and gave it a slow stirring.

When I returned to the back steps, he was looking at his watch again. His coffee cup was at his feet. "It's going to be hard. I guess I've got to."

"Go on with it."

"I've been partners with Bill for eight, going on nine years. I think he's sold his ass to Matt Turlow."

That hadn't been easy. Partners on the force, that was like being married. "You've been thinking that for a couple of days, haven't you?"

"I had a feeling."

"Since when?"

"The day he went to see Turlow alone. It was the day I was out with a cold."

"List them for me."

"He's got too much money. Yesterday I wasn't supposed to see it. He's got a roll with hundreds in it. He doesn't make that much money. I know what he makes. I've heard him talking about how he needs money to get his kid's teeth fixed. And he's distant now. Like he's holding back something. Yesterday, after he left here, he dropped me off. He said he had private business. I think that business was with Matt Turlow. And then today…" He was stumbling, running out of breath. I let him take his time. "Today, two things. He said he didn't want me along. He said…"

I guess I'd missed the point of it. "Look, I can't do anything about your problems with him. If you think he's going to double on Pike, I'll tell Pike when he calls me. There ought to be time. If the truce was set yesterday, there ought to be a week or two of peace."

"That's it. That's what I'm talking about. They haven't had that meeting yet." Bernie checked his watch. "You got the right time?"

It was 10:40. I turned the watch face so that he could compare it with his.

"The meeting is for noon."

"Where's Baylor now?"

"I don't know. Like I said, he didn't want me to back him today."

"That's all you've got? That he has more money than he should and he's distant and he doesn't want you with him?"

"It's more than that. Before he left, he unlocked the trunk and got out the clean gun." He shook his head slowly. "It's one we took off a kid on the Strip. We checked it out. Nothing on it, not even reported stolen. Usually we're pretty prompt about turning them in. But you've been there. You know now and then a clean gun can be useful."

"What make?"

"A Ruger .22. Nine-shot clip. One in the chamber makes it ten."

"He say why he took the clean gun with him?"

"I asked. Bill just looked at me. He didn't say."

I had a swallow of coffee. While the cup was at my mouth, I had a look at my watch. Ten-forty-five. "What do you think he's up to, Bernie?"

"I think he's going to waste Pike for Turlow."

It was the big possibility. "You know the plans for the meeting?"

"Pike and Turlow come alone. They meet Bill. Bill promises the meeting will be safe. He polices it."

"Where?"

"The Bricker Mansion."

"And both of them accepted it? Coming alone, no bodyguards?"

"Yes."

Odd. It didn't sound like either of them. To be that easy, that casual with their lives. There was some element missing. "What are you going to do, Bernie?"

He shook his head.

"Why bring this to me?"

"I thought you might reach Pike."

"You know better than that," I said.

He dumped the rest of his coffee in the dirt. He stood and kept his eyes from meeting mine. "I've done all I can."

"And that's it as far as you're concerned?"

He nodded. I watched the nod from the side. He placed the cup on the step without turning toward me. "I've got to go."

He went out of sight around the corner of the house. I carried both cups into the kitchen and placed them in the sink. I paced around the living room for a few minutes. It was indecision time. I was supposed to be out of it. I wasn't exactly sure what to do.

In the end, I did the only thing I could.

The Bricker Mansion was built in the early part of the century. Back in 1911 or 1912. Somewhere in there. Atlanta had been a big patent-medicine manufacturing city then. Coke had started that way, as a headache remedy. It hadn't been doing well until a druggist started adding soda water to it. And the original recipe had had cocaine in it. A soft drink with a high.

Old Man Bricker had made his fortune on Bricker's Spring Tonic. He'd built the mansion for his wife. It had cost what was a hell of a lot of money in those days. Maybe as much as a hundred thousand dollars. Maybe more because it had Italian marble floors and patios and there were marble fountains all around the grounds.

And then in the 1920s people stopped buying Spring Tonic in droves and Bricker went broke. The house changed hands several times in the years that followed but it was always known as the Bricker Mansion. By the 1940s, nobody wanted a stately mansion.

The last few years it had been deserted. Vandals had carted away everything that was movable and winos slept in the huge rooms in the winters and there had been at least one gang rape there last year.

Now and then there was talk that the city would condemn it and tear it down.

The mansion was in Druid Hills, that section that had been the residential area for people with money in past years. But now that part of town was zoned for apartments and complexes had been springing up around the Bricker Mansion in all directions.

There was an apartment house across the street. I pulled in there and parked my Ford out of sight behind a brick wall about ten feet high. I did a slow walk across the highway. I skirted the walk where the chain and the warning were. I slogged through the high weeds that had overgrown the grounds where the sculptured lawn had been. There was nobody parked nearby. No sign of Baylor's Plymouth. It was twenty minutes after eleven.

I avoided the flagstone walk that led to the front steps. The steps were about thirty feet wide and about twenty steps high. Beyond the stairs, there was an open porch that you could have driven a truck through. The flooring was marble and so were the low railings that bordered the porch. There was a fountain on the right side. It was clogged with leaves and muddy water. The centerpiece, whatever it had been, had been ripped off years ago.

I came up the stairs to the side of the porch. I passed the fountain and stopped at the main entrance to the mansion. The door was open, tilted and hanging on one brass hinge. I went in. There were no furnishings left. I saw a few wine bottles and a pile of human crap in one corner. A curving, beautiful staircase, about five people wide, led to the second floor.

I walked out again. I re-crossed the porch and went down the side steps. About twenty or thirty feet away, off to the side, there were some low hedges and an old oak tree. The hedges were thick enough to shield me. I sat down with my back to the oak. I had my .38 out. I placed it next to my leg and relaxed.

It was 11:30.

Bill Baylor arrived fifteen minutes later. He came straight up the flagstone walk to the porch. He carried his trenchcoat over his arm. There was a sag, a suggested weight, to the coat. He went directly into the mansion. When he returned a couple of minutes later, he wasn't carrying the trenchcoat. He stood on the porch for five or six minutes, looking around. At five of noon he walked down the flagstones to the driveway where the chain was. One car arrived exactly at noon. No one got out. Two minutes later a second car drove up. Pike got out of the first car, Turlow out of the late-arriving one.

From my perch I watched them come up the walk. Turlow and Pike side by side and Baylor bringing up the rear. Behind them, at the street level, both cars drove away.

Bill Baylor's harsh voice carried all the way to me. "I told both drivers to return in thirty minutes." Pike checked his watch. Turlow didn't.

They mounted the steps to the porch. Baylor guided them to the right, toward the fountain. As soon as they stopped near the fountain, Baylor went through the motions of patting both of them down. He did it with a I'm-sorry-as-hell manner. Apologies for both of them. He said something low, too low for me to hear, and Pike and Turlow laughed.

Bill Baylor left them still laughing and went through the main entrance into the mansion. Pike leaned against the marble railing and looked around. He swept a hand over the top of the railing and looked at it. Dusty.

A few feet away from him Matt Turlow, flashy in a red hop-sack jacket, brought a handkerchief from his breast pocket and spread it on the lip of the fountain.

They began their talk. I could catch words now and then. No complete sentences.

Two or three minutes must have passed. I guess I wasn't paying attention. I was straining too hard for words, some sense of what they were saying.

Then, suddenly, I saw a movement past Pike and Turlow. Bill Baylor stood on the porch. He'd just stepped out of the mansion. The Ruger was in his right hand, up and pointed.

I tried to catch up. I fumbled for the .38. I scrambled to my feet. I shouted, "Warden … Pike … watch out."

The Man put a hand on the railing and swung toward me. The wrong way, it was the wrong way. I was about to yell that when Bill Baylor started firing the Ruger. He burned most of the clip. The rounds were close together.

Only Pike didn't move. Then I realized Baylor wasn't firing at Pike. Six or eight rounds hit Matt Turlow and rammed him back into the fountain. He tried to pull himself up and I got a flash of his face. Blood gushed from it.

Baylor took a running step toward Turlow. He fired two more times from close range.

Pike, without looking around, brought out a belly gun and leaned over the railing toward me. It shocked me. He pulled off two rounds at me. One went wide. The other hit the oak behind me.

I ducked and ran. They didn't follow.

CHAPTER SEVENTEEN

At ten minutes of midnight, I started the bedtime charade. I turned off the TV and then I walked into the kitchen and ran the water in the wash sink for a few minutes and rinsed some glasses. The light switch was on the wall near the doorway that led to the living room. I hit the switch passing by and then, in the living room, I switched off the lamp near the TV and then the overhead light. Next the bedroom. I kept the light on while I sat on the edge of the bed for ten minutes. I flushed the john a couple of times and, returning to the bedroom, I waited a minute or two before I rammed the wall switch down and dipped the bedroom into darkness.

I slow-walked, in full darkness, into the living room again. It was all set up. It was the result of several hours of planning. What I'd do if I was in his position. What he'd think I was thinking. Both sides of it.

The Eveready 12-volt lantern was on the coffee table. I'd stacked a couple of books under it to put it at the right height. It was pointed at the front door. It was slightly off center, angled toward the right side of the door where the lock and the doorknob were.

The easy chair, usually at the end of the coffee table, I'd placed three feet to the left. It was closer to the kitchen doorway. I didn't want it directly behind the Eveready lantern.

I sat in the easy chair and tested it. I reached, without straining, and touched the rubber-covered spring switch on top of the lantern. Just a touch. Not enough to switch it on.

Fine. I placed the .38 P.P. on the arm of the chair, just forward of my right hand.

I didn't smoke. I'd left the smokes in the bedroom to make certain I wouldn't be tempted. I just sat there. It might take all night.

It had been too easy. That was the worm in my ear.

Both of them going so innocently to the meeting at the Bricker Mansion. Not trusting each other. Both afraid of a hit. And then the two of them standing around that dirty marble porch like they were five years old and waiting for Mama to bring the chocolate ice cream.

It didn't take a PhD to figure. Both men thought they knew something that the other one didn't. Each one believed he had the safe edge, that it was the other one who'd be bloodmeat by 12:15.

Matt Turlow had bought Baylor first. Only he hadn't stayed bought. Maybe the money hadn't been right. Maybe Baylor weighed it and knew that Pike was the man with the real grip on the city. The safe edge for him.

So the day before, when I'd turned the phone over to him and I'd gone out to have a drink with Franklin, Baylor had set up a meeting with Pike. It was the meeting to which he hadn't invited his partner. At that meeting, he'd offered Turlow to Pike. For cash. For cash and power and influence or whatever or any combination of those. Pike had agreed to it, the same way Turlow had agreed to it when Baylor had made the offer to him.

Turlow went to the meet sure he'd see Pike wasted. Pike went to see Turlow dead. Only Bill Baylor knew which one of them had really bought his ass.

Perhaps he'd wavered that moment on the porch. I don't think so. In the back of my head, I had a feeling that Baylor had been planning his move since the day he and Franklin had shipped P. J. Turner back to Detroit. The way to move Turlow out, the way to move close to Warden Pike.

And now Baylor was in high clover. Fat city. Except that I was still alive.

The phone had been ringing all afternoon and evening. Marcy had called. She wanted to come by and take care of me. I'd kept her away by saying I'd caught a spring cold and it might be better if I went to bed early and drank lots of juices. Those healthy things. And I'd said I'd call her in the morning to let her know how I was.

Hump'd called. He had some free time and wanted me to cruise a few bars with him and look at the spring girls. I gave him the same cold story. For a time, on the phone with him, I thought it might be good to have him back me. I'd been tempted. I talked myself out of it. Better to keep him out. He was a child with guns. He might walk into a stray round. I didn't want that on my head.

The third call was from Bernie Franklin. He'd wanted to know what happened at the Bricker Mansion. I'd been snotty. I'd said, how would I know? You think I went over there? When you, his partner, wouldn't go to the trouble? That was pushing the stick in and breaking it off. He'd sounded hurt and I'd got out of him that he hadn't been able to reach Baylor all afternoon. His wife didn't know where he was and she was worried too.

I told him it wasn't my problem and hung up on him.

The other call was from The Man.

"I assume, from the way you tried to warn me, that you had the best of intentions, Mr. Hardman."

"What are you talking about? Run that by one more time."

"What you witnessed this afternoon," Pike said.

"Me? I've been in the house all day with a bad cold."

"Is that the way you plan to play this?"

"Play what, Pike?"

"It is a wise decision," Pike said. There were a few seconds of silence. "I will see that it ends right here."

"You're talking past me. You been sniffing glue?"

"Good night, Mr. Hardman."

He hung up. He'd said good night, not goodbye.

Trust. That was the cheap-ass word. Right after the call, I replaced the 12-volt battery in the Eveready lantern and I started the planning.

It was a circle. Pike acted like he trusted me not to reveal what I knew about the afternoon. But I didn't trust him. And Bill Baylor, out there somewhere in the city, knew that his reputation and his career and the rest of his life rode with me. On trusting me not to say anything about what I knew.

Only he didn't trust me. And maybe he didn't trust Pike. Pike might get nervous about him. Might worry about him as long as I lived. As long as I might talk.

With all that bouncing about in my head I worked out the bedtime charade.

It would be better in my own landscape.

I was far into his head. I knew the way he thought. He was waiting for the deep sleep. He wanted me in the dark pit where I wouldn't have ears or eyes. I'd be easy then. Dead foolish dumb.

Two o'clock.

I wiggled my feet in my shoes.

Three o'clock.

I fought sleep.

A few minutes after three, I heard the first of it. The grit noise. Sand under a shoe. Like he'd stepped off the wet lawn and onto the walk. The dew bringing the dirt with it. Then there was the silence of hesitation. I didn't hear him mount the front steps. The next I heard of him was the lock picks. He was good, very good. Hardly a scratch as he used one pick, then another. He used a series of picks, I think. He was so good I couldn't be sure how many it took.

The scratching stopped. I leaned toward the Eveready lantern and placed a finger on the spring switch. The door was stuck. It was the spring dampness. He had to give it a good push. I felt the surge of displaced air. It was cool and there was the scent of some cologne on him and then I touched the lantern switch hard and he was in the flare of the light, blinded, blinking.

Baylor wore the trenchcoat. When the light nailed him, he was shoving the pick case in the left pocket of the coat. The coat was open down front and his right hand was in there, wrist deep in the waistband.

I said, "Dumb, dumb, Bill."

His hand came out of the coat. The Ruger was in it and he fired. One Time. Then again. He'd fired directly above the lantern.

I burned him three times. Trigger as fast as I could.

He hit the door. His hand clawed at it and missed and he fell out of the doorway and onto the porch steps.

I waited. I didn't move. I gave him a few seconds. He didn't move and there was no sound from him. I got up and walked toward him. The Ruger was on the floor just inside the door. I left it there. The Eveready lantern spilled enough light so I could see him. I squatted over him and tried for a pulse. Nothing. I stood and walked back to the doorway. I grabbed his legs and pulled him back into the living room. Half in and half out. I felt for the left pocket of the trenchcoat. I worried with it, like squeezing a grape, until the pick case fell out. I didn't touch the case.

I switched off the lantern. I carried it into the bedroom and stored it in the closet. I called the police number. I gave my name and the address and said that I had just shot a prowler. After I put the phone down, I undressed to my shorts and T-shirt. I got into bed and rolled around in it for a minute. I wrinkled the pillow. Then I got up and went back into the living room.

I sat in the easy chair with the front door still open. While I waited for the police, I ran the story through my head one more time. Sure, I knew Bill Baylor slightly. No, I didn't know why he'd want to break into my house. Maybe he'd heard some rumor I kept money in my house. Lord knows. All I know is that I woke up and heard him picking the lock. I got my piece and went into the living room. I was standing about here, in front of this chair, when he walked in. I told him to stop. He fired at me and I fired back. He went down. It was that simple.

Five or six minutes later I heard the first car pull up in front of the house. Some cruiser that had been in the area. I stood and waited.

Maybe I could make it fly. Maybe not. But I was still alive. That was a consolation prize of sorts.

AFTERWORD

Hardman is a Hard Man
By David H. Everson &
Christopher J. Everson

In 1974, a hard new private eye made his debut in a novel which
shifted the genre from the mean hot tubs of California to the
bars, back alleys, and "combat zones" of an old eastern city. The
novel received immediate critical acclaim from strange bedfel-
lows: The *New York Times* and *Mother Jones*. As in many such
novels, the private eye is a former cop who left the force under
a cloud. A veteran of the Korean War, he is forty-three years old
when we first meet him. He is unmarried, but maintains a "mean-
ingful relationship" with one woman. Their affair is marked by
tension and conflict over the P.I.'s haphazard "lifestyle". The P.I.
works with a black sidekick, a former professional athlete and
one mean dude. The private eye enjoys beer, food, and does some
fancy cooking. He follows the big league sports teams of his city,
avidly but with the required measure of cynicism. And he is
friends with an Irish cop. The private eye and the cop each have
used the other at times, but their friendship survives.

If you are wondering why anyone would write another piece
about Robert B. Parker and Spenser, stand at ease. The author
of the above mentioned novel — and the series that ensued — is

THE LAST OF THE ARMAGEDDON WARS

Ralph Dennis, and the P.I. is Jim Hardman. In a burst of a dozen paperback novels in the 1970s, Dennis created a "film noir" view of Atlanta, Georgia, that sticks in the mind. The stories are marked by gritty dialogue, wit, memorable characters, vintage private eye plotting, and some of the best descriptions of nasty violence to be found anywhere. The series is arguably the best "tough guy" material of the 1970s. If you don't believe it, go read one. If you can. Unfortunately, a Hardman is hard to find these days.

Hardman is not a rip-off or a spoof of Spenser. The similarities between the two are superficial and coincidental. Hump Evans, Hardman's black alter ego, was drawn as a character two years before Spenser's Hawk, who first appeared in *Promised Land* (1976). Hardman goes against the private eye code. His rule is: Get the money. Even at the physical level, Hardman is not Spenser. Spenser is a fitness freak; Hardman is, in fact, "softman" — slightly fat, balding, and out of shape. He could probably jog from the living room to the kitchen to get a beer, but he'd need to catch his breath before popping the tab. At a deeper level, Hardman is presented as much "harder" than Spenser, however. You'd have to peel away multiple levels of scar tissue to find any real softness in Hardman.

Dennis' Atlanta is the dark side of the New South. His exploration of the black criminal subculture, especially through the recurring character of the black boss — "The Man" — is a compelling look at the modern jungle.

The heart of the books is the portrayal of Jim's relationship with Hump Evans, the black former football player in incessant search of "trim." Their arrangement, born of self-interest, has evolved into respect and something perilously close to friendship. As Hardman put it early in the first novel, *Atlanta Deathwatch*: "If I had a friend left … it was probably Hump … But I'd never said anything like that to him. There was always the chance he didn't feel that way about me at all." Neither Jim nor

Hump can practice his chosen "profession." Hump tore up his knee in the NFL; Hardman resigned from the police force, a step ahead of being fired as the scapegoat in some departmental corruption. Jim still carries that stink around with him. Neither wants a 9 to 5 job, both are satisfied to make the odd dollar doing "favors." These favors include things Spenser would never consider (although Hawk would).

In the Hardman novels, developing Atlanta is symbolized by the Omni, "the new sports palace in Atlanta, that red-rusting, egg-carton jumble of steel that the owners assured everybody would weather into a bluish beauty of a building in time." The Omni figures in many of the scenes in the books. In *Working for the Man*, Hardman is sent by "The Man" to make an exchange of money for incriminating records. He sardonically observes, "The only event that hasn't been booked there is an exhibition of nude women wrestling in tubs of mud." On the outside, developing Atlanta might evolve into a "bluish beauty," but on the inside, where Hardman spends his time, a colorful mix of pimps, prostitutes, druggies, gamblers, hit men, politicians, and businessmen on the make provide the raw material for the series. Hardman's world often finds everyone wrestling in tubs of mud. No one comes out clean.

Jim's remaining friend on the force is the weary, honest Irish cop Art Maloney. Art is Catholic and he slightly disapproves of Hardman's unmarried relationship with his girl, Marcy: "He kept nibbling around the edges, trying to find out when we were going to get married … Aside from that, he was a good friend." Marcy was involved, inadvertently, in getting Jim rousted off the force. They reconcile, thanks to the intervention of Art and his wife, in *Atlanta Deathwatch*. The relationship continues its somewhat rocky course. In *The Golden Girl and All*, Marcy brings up a new man at the office who has asked her out. After some digs about Marcy and this man of culture and what they might do together, Hardman says, "You could take turns reading to each other in French and German." To which Marcy replies, "You are an ass."

In the first twenty pages of *Atlanta Deathwatch*, Dennis trashes as many of the "rules" of the private eye code as he can. Jim drops a case because of a severe beating, something which would simply double the determination of the conventional private eye. Not the pragmatic Hardman. "On my third drink, I felt good enough to stagger over to the phone and make two calls. The first one was to Arch Campbell. I told him I'd been called out of town suddenly and I wouldn't be able to follow up on the job." The second call goes to a drug dealer. Hardman, with Hump listening on, says he's "available." Then, with Hump acting as back-up, Hardman acts as a courier in a hard drug deal, a job so rank not even the younger dope-smoking private eyes of the '70s would touch it. In avenging his beating, Hardman fights as dirty as any hood: "I handed Ferd the cup and saucer ... Taking the cup and saucer from me was just a reflex. But as soon as he had it, I whirled toward him, ducked one shoulder, and hit him in the balls as hard as I could."

No private eye novels have portrayed so effectively the suspicion and hostility between white and black America, particularly as they exist at the margins — that is, in the worlds of gambling, prostitution, and other "victimless" crimes where blacks are suppliers and whites are consumers. Hardman and Hump often act as unwilling foot soldiers in an undeclared war between various factions of Atlanta's crime community. Hump and Jim (Huck and Jim?) together allow both sides of this conflict to be presented.

Consider first this scene at The Dew Drop Inn, a black hangout. Jim and Hump have gone there for information. "Hump pushed the door open and leaned in. At first they didn't see me behind him. The three blacks at the bar looked him over and then started to ease their looks away. But then I was uncovered and their eyes whipped back at me ... Hump moved toward the bartender. He was big, with round, thick shoulders and an oily-looking knife scar that began somewhere under the edge of his tee shirt and ran around the left side of his neck: 'Gentlemen, I'm sorry but we don't serve whites in here'. Down the bar, past another black, the big stud with the Afro from a few nights ago leaned forward and asked: 'What you stirring him for, Ad?' Hump turned very slowly and looked at him. Even when the stud with the Afro looked away he wasn't through. He was just waiting to see what would happen next."

Next, a parallel scene in a white pool hall in a rural Georgia town. "We headed for the bar. As soon as a few of the pool shooters saw us, there was a muttered 'nigger' or two, loud enough for us to hear but not loud enough to appear to be a challenge. I sat at the curved end of the bar, near the wired-in cage. Hump remained standing, on my left, between me and the length of the bar, where two young rednecks in jeans and denim jackets sat talking to the bartender. The bartender, a thin crew-cut man in a dirty half-apron, ignored us for two or three minutes. Then, wiping the bar top with a rag as he came, he edged toward us. 'Yeah?' 'Two beers.' 'We're out of beer ' 'One beer then,' I said. The bartender grinned. The gap-toothed pleasure meant he'd won had put it over on the nigger and the nigger-lover. He went over to the Coca-Cola box and got out three bottles of Bud. He opened two of them and placed them in front of the … rednecks. Slowly, as if the cap didn't want to come off, he opened the third one and brought it down to me … I lifted the beer and handed it to Hump. 'He's the thirsty one,' I said."

Hump and Jim have pretty much gotten past the race thing. But the rest of the world hasn't. In the black world, Hump watches Jim's back. In the white, Jim sees that Hump gets served. If necessary, the two take on their antagonists together.

The male banter between Hump and Jim is the source of most of the wit in the books. As might be expected, the irony of their black-white relationship is one focus. "Hump sipped his JAB. 'Might be a war.' 'You want to soldier in it?' 'Not me, boss.'"

The sharp edge of black humor is captured in this remark made by a black restaurant counterman warning another black not to mess with Hump: "'Mouth can get ass in trouble,' the counterman said. 'And ass can't even ask why.'" Sex is another source of humor. In *Atlanta Deathwatch*, Hump and Jim arrange to meet a man in a topless joint. Hump asks, "Why here?" Hardman deadpans, "You can never see enough titties."

The plots of the Hardman books involve vintage private eye material: missing daughters, straying wives, kids long gone, cops gone wrong. They are complex without being so dense as to be indecipherable. As in most good private eye novels, there is an element of mystery, but no locked room puzzles. Deduction has precious little to with the solution. Uncovering the motive for murder in Ralph Dennis novels means rounding up the "usual suspects" — greed, fear, hate.

Dennis repeatedly describes the situations Jim and Hump find themselves in as "rank." For example – SPOILER ALERT, skip this paragraph if you don't want part of the mystery in an earlier Hardman novel revealed to you — in *The Deadly Cotton Heart,* a nice young rich boy hires Jim and Hump to find his wandering wife. (Previously, Jim had pretended to be a hitman interested in a contract to kill this man.) It turns out that she is a former hooker, perjurer, and accessory after the fact to murder. And she's dead and buried in a muddy field shortly after the search starts. It is apparent that the rich man doesn't know anything about the woman he was married to for six years. Hardman has to tell him the truth. Rank.

As the series progresses, there is a subtle shift in the stance of Hardman and Hump. It is too strong to suggest they become knights. But ethical choices do seem to matter more. In *Hump's First Case*, Hump takes on a client that Hardman rejects. The job is too rank even for him — some rich parents want him to find their daughter who is in the worst kind of trouble. But Hardman has witnessed her participation in a robbery/murder. Their disagreement ends in this exchange. Hardman asks, "'Want to bet on that?' Hump shook his head. 'I don't bet with close-in people.' It was as close as he could come to saying friends. 'I'm going to help her if I can, Jim.' 'I figured as much.1 'Hard feelings?' 'Not a one.'" Not from a hard man.

As presented in the early pages of *Atlanta Deathwatch*, Jim Hardman is a classic tough guy — an amoral Sam cum Spade for the 1970s. No job is too rank for Hardman as long as it isn't too difficult and it pays. Hump is a stereotype: a trim-chasing black stud. However, as the softcover series proceeds, cracks in the hard cover of the protagonists appear. Although they deny it, Hardman and Hump both have a moral compass beyond the dirty dollar. Consider *The Buy Back Blues*; Hardman takes on a low-paying job for a waitress whose husband is missing. "Neither of us wants to do more than we have to do to make a living. The bare minimum. The hundred dollars from Barbara wasn't more than drinks and meals for the two days of the hunt. It was, I guess, what you call a favor, favor."

Dennis' writing skill is revealed in the way he describes violence. It is never pretty and it always hurts. "The black hard mean was running in him. He was at the point where he didn't much give a shit about how much he got hurt if he could give back more of it than he got … Blue leisure suit wanted that it was enough. He started his dive for the floor. Hump didn't want it to be that easy. Hump caught him by the shoulder and righted him. He brought his knee up at the same time pulling the man's head down. His face hit Hump's knee and he gurgled and fell away."

Ralph Dennis has created a violent world in the Atlanta of the 1970s. This series has everything the follower of the genre looks for: a rich locale; sharply drawn characters and complex relationships; biting, cynical dialogue; enough plot and mystery to drive the stories forward at a continuous pace; and convincing violence. In addition, Dennis takes us into the world of black/white relationships and and the criminal subculture of black

Atlanta. The twelve books have a unity rarely found in tough guy novels. They are superior to any competing work of the 1970s.

This essay was originally published in the summer 1986 issue of *Hardboiled* magazine. David Everson was a member of the founding faculty members at Sangamon State University, now the University of Illinois in Springfield, where first served as a professor of political science and later as an associate chancellor. He was also the two-time Shamus Award nominated author of seven "Robert Miles" private eye novels: *Recount, Rebound, Rematch, Instant Replay, A Capitol Killing, Suicide Squeeze* and *False Prophets.*

Christopher Everson worked for the Illinois State Legislature for 12 years and has been at the Illinois Department of Transportation for almost 16 years. He lives in Springfield, Illinois. Chris is married to Anne and they have two children, Bethany and David.

AFTERWORD

Ralph Dennis, the Science Fiction Writer? By David H. Everson

I got a sinking feeling when I saw the hand-lettered sign which said: RALPH DENNIS MEMORIAL BOOKRACK. The used books in the rack were a mix of mysteries—not all hard-boiled. But then, he had written me that along with Ross Thomas and James Crumley, he liked Jonathan Gash and Charles McCarry. I shrugged. Maybe it's an inside joke, I told myself. I called my son Chris over and showed him the sign.

He said: "What does it mean?"

"He may have died," I said, but I really could not believe he was gone.

We were in the Oxford Too—a used bookstore hoping to finally meet Ralph Dennis.

I had admired his Hardman series and had corresponded with him. On a rainy Atlanta day in 1987, on our way to Florida, we had missed him—it had been his day off.

I walked over to the counter with the books Chris and I had picked out. "When will Ralph Dennis be in?" I asked with some apprehension.

The female clerk looked puzzled. She turned to the male who was working at a computer. "He doesn't work here anymore, does he?"

The male clerk looked up at me and frowned. We were less than an underhand toss from the bookrack. "The science fiction writer?"

I didn't correct him. Somehow, the mistake seemed symbolic of Ralph's late career.

"He died about six months ago," the clerk said matter-of-factly.

I nodded. I had never even talked to him, but I felt the loss.

I had first read Ralph's PI novels set in Atlanta in about 1974. His work and Robert B. Parker's started at about the same time. Especially in the early books, you had to get past the lurid covers which suggested a men's adventure series. The books were tough. gritty, and funny. They dealt with racial tensions as well as any fiction I knew.

I loved the titles: *The Deadly Cotton Heart, The One Dollar Rip-Off, The Last of the Armageddon Wars.* The Atlanta locale was sharply drawn. And best of all—there were lots of Hardmans. They seemed to come out in bunches—none of this waiting for a year for a new one. I devoured them as quickly as they appeared—and often reread them. They were reviewed favorably in such diverse publications as *Mother Jones* and *The New York Times.*

Ralph also published two non-Hardman paperback originals and one hardcover, *MacTaggart's War,* a big caper novel with a great firefight scene—set during WWII (the novel has been substantially revised and republished by Brash Books as *The War Heist*). Then suddenly the flow of his work ceased. Every so often Chris and I would say: "Wonder when Ralph Dennis will publish another Hardman?"

Never, it turned out.

Flash forward to the mid-80s. I had taken tentative steps toward my own mystery writing career. I was eager to break into print. I had subscribed to Wayne Dundee's *Hardboiled,* but short story writing was not in me. Chris and I concocted the idea of writing a piece lauding Dennis. Dundee knew Dennis's work, liked it. and thought the idea was a good one. For some basic facts. Chris tracked down an article on Dennis that had appeared in an Atlanta newspaper.

The article that we wrote appeared in *Hardboiled* in Summer 1986. We said that the Hardman series was arguably the best 'tough guy' material of the '70s. I think we were being conservative. The Hardman novels stack up against the best PI fiction. Ever. Yet most readers, and even many PI writers, are unaware of Ralph Dennis's work.

About that time, I learned from a short piece in *Mystery Scene* that Dennis worked at Oxford Too in Atlanta. I looked up the address in the Atlanta phone book and I sent Dennis a copy of the piece.

I received a long letter in reply. It began: "Thanks for the magazine. The article about the Hardman books might have been a bit kinder than the books…written in two months each…deserved. As I remember I did ten pages a day for a month and I had a first draft and then a rewrite…ten pages a day… and then I shipped it off to New York. To paraphrase Fitzgerald, who wrote that there were no third acts in American lives…I guess I'd say there are no third drafts in paperback originals."

Ralph went on to say that he stopped doing the Hardmans because of "the special burnout that shows up in series writers." He wrote about his recent frustrations. "You're only as bankable as your last book," he wrote, reporting that after *MacTaggart's War* —which sold eight or nine thousand copies —he had penned five books "and nobody wanted any of them."

He described each briefly. One was on college basketball. I happened to be writing a novel on the same theme at that time. I would love to read them all.

He had finished a new book for which he had hopes. He wrote: "It's titled *Dust in the Heart.* It's about a sheriff in a small town in the triangle area of North Carolina on the hunt for a child-molester murderer. I like the book. I've taken a lot of time over it. Now we'll see what the body-eaters up there in New York think." He promised to let me know what came of it.

One of the books in the Hardman series had been reprinted by Pinnacle Books. He wrote: "I thought the idea was to reprint four or five of the ones I liked best … then the editor moved … and the other people at Pinnacle weren't interested." He complained about "literary slavery." Pinnacle had gone into bankruptcy. "We asked for the rights back. The judge has ruled that the contracts are part of the assets of Pinnacle. Hell, I could be sold off to the highest bidder with no say in the matter. Wasn't slavery outlawed?"

He said he was going to send our article to his agent.

I replied to his letter, telling him about my own writing.

Then came our failed attempt to see him in the spring of '87. In June, I received another letter. It came to me indirectly because he had misplaced my address. His luck was still bad — *Dust* had *almost* sold. He was sorry we had missed connections. He thought someone at the store should have pointed us in the direction of his "watering hole." He wanted another copy of the *Hardboiled* article—a low-budget Hardman film was maybe in the works. "Iffy," he said. I rushed the copy off to him, hoping it was not too late. He promised to send me copies of some of the Hardmans I lacked.

In August of '87, I nervously sent him a copy of my first novel, a paperback original entitled *Recount*, which had a brief tribute to Hardman and Hump buried in it.

I never heard from him again.

I don't know any of the details of his death, so I don't know if the weight of the rejections contributed somehow.

To me, Dennis was the Joe DiMaggio of private eye writers. It seemed he did it effortlessly. I do know that no one, and I include giants like Robert B. Parker and John D. MacDonald, has ever had a better run — a longer hit streak—than Ralph Dennis did in the Hardman series. There was no drop-off in quality as the series continued. It will be a crime if this series is not made available to contemporary PI readers.

Dust in my heart. Ashes in my throat.

Ralph Dennis—the science fiction writer?—he doesn't work here anymore.

This essay was published in 1993 in the anthology *The Fine Art of Murder.*

Made in the USA
Middletown, DE
03 August 2019